CLOUD OF EVIL

Fiona strolled along beside the Loch, her hair now glowing so brightly in the sunlight that Donald forgot the frustration of his attempted lovemaking. In three days she would be his wife. He lay on the grass and watched her, beaming happily at her coy laughter.

Suddenly, a cloud blotted the sun out. An unutterable sensation of horror came over Donald. He stared after Fiona. Incredibly, her warm, healthy face had become dead-white and pasty. Her feet turned robot-like towards the Loch's bank. "Fiona!" Donald screamed.

She heard nothing. Black water lapped her shoes. She walked straight into it, as if stricken dumb—an erect, solitary figure proceeding deliberately to a suicide's death . . .

THE CURSE OF RATHLAW

PETER SAXON

PRESTIGE BOOKS • NEW YORK

THE CURSE OF RATHLAW

PRESTIGE BOOKS INC. • 18 EAST 41ST STREET
NEW YORK, N.Y. 10017

Chapter One

The crudely built wooden bothy stood isolated, clinging to a hillside overlooking the Black Loch.

Remote, ramshackle and decaying, it was the kind of hut in which even a tramp might have hesitated to spend more than one night, even for lack of better shelter. As a permanent residence it could have recommended itself to no one but an extreme eccentric.

About it mist curled. A clammy, vaporous shroud hid the hilltop and the sky of late afternoon. Below the level of the bothy the mist was thinner, but the gorse-and-heather-clad slope was deserted, its steep incline broken only by scattered clumps of dark bracken.

Lower still visibility again decreased, because at its foot the hillside plunged into the secretive, almost sinister, shadows of the glen. And that gloom was relieved only by a pallid glimmer on the glassy black surface of the loch. Black Loch.

This primitive, uncultivated terrain, silent in somber grandeur, adjoined the far-reaching domain of the Laird of Rathlaw. Only ancient maps defined the boundary, which was marked neither by hedge nor by fence.

Surrounding the Laird's castle, situated in the center of his domain, were the crofts and sheepfolds of his hard-working tenants. Even they, accustomed to the bleak remoteness of life in the Scottish Highlands, were glad to have neighbors.

But no crofter or shepherd wished to be a neighbor of Fergus Trayle, the Hermit of Black Loch.

Even a stranger entering the hermit's bothy would immediately have found this easy to understand. The stench of stale food overcame even the acrid smoke of the smoldering peat fire. Then there was the odor of Fergus Trayle himself, as he sprawled in silent self-communion beside that fire . . .

Fergus Trayle set little value on personal hygiene. He was a gaunt, raw-boned man, over six feet tall. His hair was untrimmed and unkempt, as were his mustache and beard. Originally that hair had been brown, but, overlaid by dirt, it was now a dull black. And sweat had glued it into tangled tufts.

The teeth exposed when his sensual lips parted in mute rumination were unbrushed and discolored. His breath was malodorous.

He was wearing a long, dark grey garment reminiscent of a monk's cassock, but in his sprawling posture it had worked itself up to reveal his calves and ankles, grey with the ingrained grime of years.

His deep-sunken eyes were oddly assorted. The black pupils were of different sizes, the irises unmatched in color—one mottled brown-and-green, the other slate-grey.

This phenomenon gave his stare a baleful and powerfully hypnotic quality; even his casual glance unnerved people—except, of course, for the eccentric and depraved, those initiates who made periodic pilgrimages to his dark and secret shrine . . .

Suddenly, with an uncouth grunt, Fergus Trayle stirred from his abstract meditations beside the peat fire. His weird eyes focused. Standing, he braced his broad shoulders and flexed his arms to restore the circulation. The cassock alone would not suit the deed he'd been broodingly planning. He took from an iron hook on the wall an old woolen plaid and draped it around him. When he stepped out of his bothy he looked like a Highland shepherd of the old days.

For a moment, in the open air, he spared an upward glance at the wet, wreathing mist. That mist, thickening and spreading to lower levels, was as welcome as the darkness of night.

He moved down the steep slope, but not all the way down towards the glen and the loch. Instead he crossed the brae and loped steadily towards the boundary of the Laird of Rathlaw's domain.

Thanks to the spreading mist, his succulent prey would certainly be caught unawares.

Jean Patterson was 19 and generally acknowledged to be bonnie, a word that conveyed to her far more than the Sassenach 'pretty.' For 'bonnie' was especially Ian Mather's word for her, and Ian, 23 and braw, was the lad Jean loved and planned to marry. Ready to leave Rathlaw Castle at five o'clock, it was Ian for whom she had paid a half-hour's attention to hair, cheeks and glowing eyes, making herself as beautiful as any kinswoman of the Laird.

Jean was in fact only a kitchenmaid in Rathlaw Castle, subordinate to most of the Laird's domestics. But she would very soon be installed in Ian's home, and that was the status she wanted. Ian was the only child of a widowed mother and he ran the rented family croft single-handed. Mrs. Mather welcomed her, not simply as an extra hand for domestic tasks, but because in Jean she saw an endearing person essential to her only son's happiness.

Jean was softly humming a lilting song of serene anticipation when she left the Castle to meet her Ian. Mist had spread down from the hills, but so far was thin in the vicinity of the Castle. Such mists could disperse as quickly as they gathered, or could overtake one even if the weather was clear when one set out. So whatever conditions prevailed at the outset, some risk was involved. A person who waited for a guarantee of perfect weather throughout a journey could wait forever.

Anyway, she had only to follow the road of beaten earth and stones, which was used by the Laird's vehicles, in order to keep in the right direction for her rendezvous with Ian.

The picturesque old building she left behind her, with its sharply pointed conical corner turrets, would have intrigued tourists and enchanted historians, but it was too familiar for Jean to give it a backward glance. She began trudging the crudely-made road —to her strong young legs and sensibly-shod feet, no hardship. Besides, she was buoyantly happy. The road petered out short of the boundary of the Laird's estate. Its continuance would have reached the Black Glen and Black Loch and would have been little used due to the fear the superstitious had of these somber places. Even Jean was touched by that fear. Yet she strode on. Before she had covered much ground, the mist thickened, and she began groping her way across the roadless countryside. When a human figure loomed ahead in the mist, she gave a glad smile. Here was Ian coming to meet her.

But the blurred silhouette coming towards her was not Ian. Only when Jean had covered a quarter of the intervening distance and the figure had covered a third of it could she be sure. And then she came to an abrupt, unsteady stop. The person coming quickly towards her was a bearded man, clad in garments of a kind Ian would never have worn.

This in itself was no cause for alarm. Even in the cities, Jean had heard, many young men now went unshaven and in the Highlands beards and plaids were common enough among older men.

Jean stopped not because the man wasn't Ian, not because he was a stranger. Indeed, he was not exactly a stranger to her, although she had never seen him before. She could now see him well enough to be able to identify him. His appearance had long been the subject of gossip and sinister speculation. The man now coming swiftly towards her must be the odd recluse generally referred to as the Hermit of Black Loch.

The thought immediately quickened the beat of her heart.

Fergus Trayle . . . about whom such frightening stories were told in the Castle servants' quarters. Stories which alleged that, although no human being had ever been seen to visit him, he was not really alone in his bothy.

On occasions, crofters or shepherds venturing nearer than usual to his hillside retreat had heard strange sounds rising from it and lingering over it, as if reluctant to fade away like the sounds made by mortal men. Sounds of singing made by more than

9

one voice, and varying from a monotonous wailing to a chorus of demoniac glee.

Of these things the explanation whispered among the gossips steeped in the old lore of Highland occultism, the product of centuries of brooding in the solitude of misted hills or shadowed glens, was one all-embracing Gaelic word.

The comment was: "Buidseahcd!"

And, for lack of a more plausible explanation, 'Witchcraft' was the one most generally accepted.

But these knowing whispers were not the only reason why Jean suddenly turned and took to flight when the Hermit came near enough for identification.

At close range his appearance alone was enough to frighten even a girl who had never heard of him. His unkempt condition, the evil grin parting his bearded lips. . . . Plainly, it was not his intention to pass Jean by. His run had been aimed directly at her, to bar her progress; had made her its objective.

The road behind her was now not safe to return to, for he could follow her too easily on it. Only in the wider expanse of countryside was there the prospect of safety. If she could get far enough away, deep enough into the mist, to lose him!

After that moment of shock, Jean veered to her right and bolted, with no destination in mind, her intention only to put distance between herself and that figure of terror.

When sure she was out of danger she might revert to her original direction—or even head back for the Castle. The latter would mean returning to the road. He might lie in ambush somewhere along it. Such plans flew through her mind as she ran, and both were overly optimistic.

Before she had travelled a dozen yards she heard him pursuing her—and overtaking her.

She could hear the swishing of his feet and legs through the undergrowth. And, bizarrely, the sound of his deep voice in exultant song.

Even in her panic-stricken flight she recognised the tune as that of the traditional 'White Cockade.' The words were undistinguishable.

And when, seconds later, they became distinct, she not only knew that he must be close behind her, but had frightening confirmation of his aim in pursuing her.

They were not the authentic words belonging to that title and tune, but words to which the tune had often been sung. She had heard them before, but not in this terrifying situation.

They were the words of a ribald ditty composed early in the nineteenth century by 'Blind Rob', a sightless fiddler living near Crieff. They concerned the excuse offered by an opportunist butcher who had taken improper advantage of a lady customer.

" 'Frae flesher Rab that lived in Crieff
A bonnie lassie wanted to buy some beef;
He took her in his arms and down she did fa',
And the wind blew the bonnie lassie's plaidie
awa' . . .' "

Panting from exertion and panic, her heart pounding and her lungs straining her rib-cage, Jean realized now that she had no chance of by-passing the Hermit.

And the words of the song hammered at her in mocking menace.

She had heard drunken men singing the outrageous old words, so she knew the gist of the subsequent verses. Of the consequences for the bonnie lassie—and her shotgun wedding to the opportunist butcher. And the chorus her pursuer was chanting in exultant innuendo left Jean in no doubt of his intentions once his clutch should fasten on her.

". . . *Her plaidie awa', her plaidie away' . . .*
He took her in his arms and down she did fa'—
And the wind blew the bonnie lassie's plaidie
awa' . . ."

Jean's reasoned decision to keep running straight ahead, as her best chance of keeping out of his reach, did not last long. As the swishing of his feet through the undergrowth became faster and louder, she panicked again. Instinctively she veered in the direction of the nearest building that could provide a haven—the Castle. It was a long way away now, but not as far as the nearest croft. Not nearly as far away as Ian must still be.

Back towards the Castle and the road she ran. Almost at once her pursuer also changed direction. Within seconds, it seemed, he was overtaking her again.

Her breathing was now a series of racking gasps. Pain stabbed at her side. Her run became an ungainly stumbling over uneven ground. In her blind haste she tripped over a heather root and went sprawling face-down.

Her impetus kept her moving in a dizzy roll, clutching with a frantic instinct for a hand-hold on the heather.

12

As she found a grip she came to a slithering stop, with her skirt dragged up above her knees and her heels digging in for an additional braking effect.

She was left sprawling giddily on her back, anchored by one hand and one heel, the other hand and foot flung out so that she was spreadeagled.

And then her dizzy eyes saw the silhouette of the Hermit, now at close range and distorted in outline as he bore down on her in a crouch.

She raised her head in a desperate attempt to evade him and take to flight again. But the stare of his eerily unmatched eyes paralyzed her, made evasion and flight physical impossibilities. The bearded lips opened to reveal his discolored teeth. And on a gust of foul breath came the taunting, gloating chant:

". . . *And the wind blew the bonnie lassie's plaidie awa'* . . ."

The words, and the grin on the face looming nearer and nearer above her, stimulated Jean into a spasm of action. Her trembling hands pushed at her skirt to force its hem down over her knees. But that defensive movement was ended by a grimy, immensely strong hand.

It grabbed at one of her wrists, enclosed it, then grabbed the other and held both wrists imprisoned. Leaving him one hand free to—

The rip of cloth was followed by a low, evil chuckle and a resumption of the thick-voiced chant:

". . . *and the wind blew the bonnie lassie's plaidie awa'* . . ."

Even the elements contributed to her horror. Because, unnoticed before, the mist which had helped him to trap her now thinned as if specially to bring the nightmarish face into sharp, petrifying clarity.

The face was etched with a beast's lust. The hand imprisoning her wrists leaned heavily on her ribcage, pinning her down.

Chapter Two

Taking advantage of the rapidly improving visibility as he knelt over her, the Hermit studied her with a widening grin of self-congratulation on her youth and attractiveness.

When his great hand moved again and his foul breath was a sickening miasma around her face, Jean's sudden wild shrieks tore through the dissipating mist and across the bleak countryside.

"Ian—Ian! Help! Ian! Ian!" Instinctively she screamed for her lover.

Snarling the Hermit clapped his hand down across her mouth. Her lips broke and bled. But although almost fainting from terror and the nearness of his vile odor, Jean writhed and bit.

When her teeth penetrated a finger he snarled another obscenity and snatched his hand away. With her mouth freed, she shrilled another scream for help. Then the weight of him crushed down on her and she was totally engulfed.

Almost smothered by the loathsome body, she dimly heard a distant shout. Jean's heart leaped. After a pause, during which her flesh shrank from the imminent outrage, the shout was repeated. A little nearer, a little louder—in comprehensible words.

"Hey, there! Where are ye? Are ye hairt? We cannae help if ye no'—"

The voice spurred her into a frenzied struggle that needed both of the Hermit's hands to subdue. And with the removal of that gagging hand she drew a panting breath and another desperate scream tore from her.

"Here! This way! Help me! Oh, God—"

The Hermit had lost all restraint, ravenously intent on making sure of his prey and his purpose before he could be thwarted. And it was because he could not resist his appetite's urgent clamor for satisfaction that he lost his chance to escape.

Jean, again almost submerged under his frantic onslaught, did not see the man who a few yards away paused briefly on sighting the source of the screams, then loudly summoned his two companions.

"This way, lads! Come on—!"

And he himself dashed straight to the rescue.

The Hermit's first intimation of his arrival was the grasp of a muscular hand on his matted hair. When his head was dragged up and back by that first grip, another hand got hold of him by the beard, and by their combined strength he was hauled bodily away from his semi-conscious victim.

Falling, he slewed sideways. The hand he put out to save himself kept him propped up as he sprawled

15

dizzily, mentally absorbing the shock of what had happened to him at the crucial moment.

That it *had* been the crucial moment the man who had so abruptly intervened could see merely by looking at him. And as he stood there, with fists clenched, glowering down at the snarling Hermit, he was joined by his two companions.

One carried a pruning-hook. His glance passed from the bearded man to the disarrayed girl—who now, her rescuers at hand, slumped into complete unconsciousness.

The man with the pruning-hook gave a furious bellow.

"It's Jeannie! Wee Jeannie frae the Castle!" He scowled at Fergus Trayle, lifting the pruning-hook threateningly. "By God, if it was left tae me, I'd mak' sure ye'd no' be a danger tae a lassie iver again . . ."

He took a step towards the Hermit, the hook still raised, but the third arrival, a younger man, stopped him.

"Let the Laird deal wi' him." He gave the shaggy man a keen scrutiny. "Hey! This must be the Hermit. The fella' they talk aboot. The Hermit o' Black Loch!" Rather uneasily he added: "Sure, let the Laird deal wi' him."

Angus, the middle-aged man, grunted. "Aye, ye're right, nae doot. Though I'd tak' mah hook tae the skunner if he were the De'il himself. But you two lads get hold o' him, tak' him tae the truck and tie him up, while I see tae the lassie. Tak' the hook, one o' ye, tae keep him in order."

Duncan, the brawny young man who had first reached the spot, accepted the pruning-hook with

16

relish. He moved to stand over the Hermit, followed by the other young man.

Before they dragged the Hermit to his feet, Angus gave them a warning.

"Mind what I tell ye noo', Duncan an' Colin! Ye'll forget all aboot seein' the lassie in this state. We'll talk tae the Laird in private, an' when she comes roon' she shall no' be shamed by what we've seen here. Ye understand?"

Both men nodded. Then they bent over the Hermit. Big and strong as they were, he would have been a difficult proposition but for the pruning-hook. Snarling obscenities, he pushed Colin out of the way, and while Colin was staggering, tried to dodge Duncan and bolt.

Duncan, however, moved with a surprising speed. His right arm shot out and the pruning-hook swept across at throat level to bar the Hermit's way. The Hermit had a choice between coming to a sudden stop—or having his throat cut. When he chose to stop, Duncan looked disappointed.

"So ye wullnae gi'e me an excuse!" he commented. "Colin, tak' hold o' that hair of his. That's right—keep his chin up. Then if he tries tae get awa' again, I'll gi'e him the fastest shave a man iver had. An' it wullnae be bloodless."

Ignominiously, with his head tilted back in Colin's grip, the Hermit was marched back to the road. With the mist gone, he could see there the Land Rover from which the Laird's three employees had leapt on hearing the girl's screams.

But the two young men and their prisoner did not reach the road without incident.

While Duncan was marching beside him, with the

17

pruning-hook ready, the Hermit gave him a steady, unblinking, baleful stare.

No longer was he snarling. But even with his head tilted painfully back he held Duncan's eyes with that glare. And before a dozen yards had been covered, the hypnosis had effect.

As though suddenly weary, Duncan let his right arm fall. Then, with the pruning-hook hanging at his side, he turned away and walked off at a tangent, leaving Colin alone with the prisoner.

Colin shouted after him. "Duncan! Where are ye awa', man!"

There was no response. It was only when Colin shouted again, at twice the volume, that Duncan stopped. Then he shook himself, like someone coming out of a walking sleep. He turned vaguely. Colin gave a third rousing shout.

"Duncan! Where are yeer wits, man? Come here wi' that hook—"

Duncan lost his dazed look and hurried back to assist Colin with the struggling Hermit. Red with shame at how he had been used, he thrust the blade of the pruning-hook right up to the man's weird eyes. He put his left forefinger to his mouth to wet it, then passed the fingertip over his own eyelid.

"Ye'll no' put the evil eye on me again!" he said furiously. "Ye've just seen me guard against it. But if ye try again, I'll have yeer ain een oot o' yeer head with this hook!"

The blade was so dangerously near to him that even the Hermit was intimidated. But during the remainder of the march to the Land Rover, Colin moistened his own eyelids with saliva for protection.

The two young men did not rely upon that charm

18

alone, however. Before dumping their prisoner in the back of the Land Rover they tied his wrists together behind his back with thick rope, bound his ankles securely—and, as an extra safeguard, blindfolded him with a thick, oily rag.

Almost immediately after the Hermit had been dealt with, Angus arrived carrying Jean. He had secured her torn skirt with a safety-pin and rearranged the rest of her clothing. The girl was not yet conscious. But as Angus made to lift her into the Land Rover, she stirred, muttering.

"We'll have tae put her in the back," Angus said, "so that I can keep an eye on her. But gi'e me that hook and I'll keep an eye on oor ither passenger as weel. Hold the lassie a while, Duncan!"

Angus exchanged Jean for the pruning-hook, climbed into the back of the Land Rover, then waited for Duncan to pass the girl up to him. Before the young man could do so, however, her eyelids fluttered. She gave a frightened moan and cringed in Duncan's grasp.

"It's all right, Jeannie," he said soothingly. "Everything's all right. Ye're wi' friends—"

He was interrupted by a shout from along the road. Colin turned and gave an exclamation.

"Och! Look who's here. Jeannie, ye'll be all right noo'. Here's yeer Ian!"

He waved, and Ian Mather came running along the road to the stationary Land Rover. It was not until he came around the side of the vehicle that he saw and recognised Jean. Then he started forward in alarm.

"Jeannie! What's wrong with her? She didnae arrive, so I came along all this way tae find out—"

Angus leaned out of the Land Rover.

"Dinnae fash yeersel', lad! Get up in front wi' Duncan an' Colin. I'll tak' care o' the lassie—an' tell ye what happened while we're on oor way back tae the Castle. The Laird sent us tae gi'e Widow Lachlan some help on her croft. We were on oor way back when we haird the lassie . . . But jump in, lad! She's awake . . ."

Jean opened her eyes fearfully, but when she saw that she was among friends, a flood of relieved tears flowed. Ian took her in his arms, caressing and soothing her. Angus waited patiently until the young couple drew apart. Then he said dourly:

"Och—ye'll have time enough f'r that! Help the lassie into the truck, Ian—an' get in yeersel'—"

A couple of minutes later the Land Rover, with three unexpected extra passengers aboard, was speeding back along the rough road to the Castle.

The mist had gone, but the shadows of dusk were now creeping in across the deserted countryside.

It would be dark when the Hermit was brought to account before the Laird.

Chapter Three

Sir Alastair Rathlaw was a man of middle height and of late middle-age. He had aquiline features which might have suggested an aristocratic arrogance had they not been belied by the habitual twinkle in his blue eyes and the sensitive curve of his mouth.

His tenants and dependants knew that the eyes and mouth were the true indicators of his character, which was generous and sympathetic. Loyalty to him was due to no mere tradition nor formal duty; it was inspired by the knowledge that he had more regard for the obligations of his station in life than for its privileges.

Among great landowners, the Laird did not rate as a rich man. His acreage was extensive, but for pasturage granted to small-scale sheep farmers he made no charge and the meager rents of his crofts were returned to the tenants in the form of maintenance services. The upkeep of the Castle was paid for by the profits of his personal farm.

The system prevailing in Sir Alastair's domain was feudal, but with the best features of feudalism, which took the whole scattered populace under the shield of a benovolent paternalism.

So when a female member of Sir Alastair's staff, of his own household, was subjected to outrage by a trespasser, the Laird did not think of sending the miscreant all the way to Edinburgh or Glasgow, to be charged and tried by due process of the law. To have done so would have been to expose the girl to embarrassment and humiliation, both as a witness in court and in the subsequent press reports.

Moreover, the insult and the injury had in effect been inflicted on everyone under the Castle roof. It threatened the sense of security and protection the Laird had promised to tenants of even the remotest crofts.

Obviously the person to uphold justice in this case

was the Laird himself—so it was the Laird who sat in judgment in the great, echoing chamber which was the banqueting hall.

As always, while in the Castle, he was wearing traditional Highland dress, kilt, and tartan stockings, with the *skean dhu*, the traditional black knife, tucked into the top of the right one.

Beside the Laird's high-backed chair stood his only son, Donald, in a tweed suit of lovat green. Father and son were positioned beneath the old minstrels' gallery, and the Hermit was brought before them, still blindfolded.

Jean Patterson, after confirming the story told by her three rescuers, had been sent to bed in the care of an older woman of the domestic staff. Her lover, Ian Mather, had insisted on being present when the criminal was sentenced. Only a stern command from the Laird had prevented him from executing summary justice with his own hands.

Now he stood to one side in the background, fuming with rage as Angus, Duncan and Colin brought the prisoner in, with the additional escort of two men carrying shotguns. The Laird had made no comment when told why the Hermit had been blindfolded, but neither had he ordered the blindfold removed.

Now, as the Hermit—still with his hands bound behind him—was brought to a halt between Angus and Duncan, the Laird's nostrils distended in distaste. Even at that distance, the Hermit's vile odor reached him.

To think that such dirt and filth should have forced itself upon a helpless, innocent young girl . . . the disgust on the Laird's face was reflected in the eyes of his son.

Judging the criminal was a formality. The Laird

22

eyed the man coldly and said with bleak sternness:

"My men call you 'the Hermit,' but presumably you have a name. What is it?"

The reply came in a voice charged with venom: "My name is Fergus Trayle. It's a name you will do well to remember unless you set me free at once."

The creature's speech was surprisingly precise and unaccented.

The Laird ignored the threat. Icily he said: "You were caught in the act of committing an abominable outrage on a girl of my household. Have you anything to say before I pass sentence on you?"

"*You* pass sentence on *me?*" The prisoner gave a harsh, sardonic laugh. "I realize I am being addressed by the Laird of Rathlaw, but evidently you are far from realizing the kind of man you are presuming to judge! Your ignorance is pitiful—and at the moment blissful. But if you should dare to give me reason to enlighten you, you will regret it as long as you live!"

Some of the men guarding the prisoner glanced at one another uneasily. Duncan and Colin again moistened their eyelids furtively with saliva, muttering prayers under their breath. There was a frightening confidence in the Hermit's threat, an intimation of his command which recalled all the whispered gossip about him—and reminded Duncan and Colin of what had happened just before he had been blindfolded. If he were given real cause to hate anyone—

But the Laird refused to be intimidated.

"You are a disgusting blackguard in every respect," he said caustically. "You contaminate this place even by breathing in it. You inflicted your vile

23

person on a girl under my protection. You behaved, in fact, like a dog in rut, and I am going to have you treated as a savage animal. You are going to be soundly flogged and then thrown off my land. And if you ever set foot upon it again that flogging will be repeated."

"You—" The Hermit let loose a flood of obscene profanity.

Angus stepped forward.

"If ye'll excuse me suggestin' it, Sir Alastair," he said dourly. "I'd like tae volunteer tae dae the floggin'."

The Laird gave a grim smile. "I'm sure you would do it with enthusiasm, Angus," he replied. "But I think a younger man would have more physical energy for the task. And there's a young man here with a personal score to settle." The Laird looked past Angus and asked: "Would you be willing to carry out the sentence, Ian?"

The answer exploded from the young man. "Willing? I'd give all I possess to get my hands on that—"

The Laird shook his head. "Not your hands, Ian. I could not allow you to befoul yourself by touching this man with your bare hands. But I'll give you a hunting whip. It will be burnt afterwards, since it could hardly be used for anything else after contact with such disgusting flesh. Duncan! Colin! Take him out."

With his feet scuffling along the floor, the Hermit was dragged bodily out by the two stalwart young men. All the way along the great hall, torrents of vituperation poured from him, and by the time they had got him out into the courtyard both Duncan and Colin were sweating.

24

Two other men fetched a wooden bench, across which the Hermit was flung. Donald brought one of his father's hunting whips and handed it to Ian.

The evening was dark. Some illumination came into the castle courtyard from several undraped windows. Thoughtfully, however, Donald strolled across to his parked sports car and switched on the headlamps to spotlight the scene.

The Hermit writhed blindly, belly-down on the bench, fighting to regain his feet. Duncan grabbed him by the scruff of his neck and held him down while Colin wrenched the cassock-like garment off his shoulders and dragged it down to expose his grimy back.

The two men stepped clear. Ian had examined the whip and found it satisfactory. The thick cane handle was firmly grasped in his hand; it terminated in a plaited leather thong which ended with a lash of twisted cord.

He went forward. Into the Hermit's ears he muttered: "I'm going to make you scream as she screamed, you animal!"

And he did. Stony-faced, he swung the whip and brought the thong whistling down. There was a cracking sound as the lash hit flesh—and the Hermit's profanity was cut off with a gasp.

Blood soon streamed from the filth-encrusted back. The Hermit was screaming like a woman and writhing like a serpent. He wriggled until his frantic struggles broke the rope which bound his wrists. Ian would have continued lashing him until he lost consciousness, but at the Laird's nod Duncan and Colin dashed forward and dragged the young man back.

Then, watched by a dozen pairs of eyes, the

Hermit got a grip with his hands on the bench and pushed himself half-upright, sobbing and snuffling with pain. To stand straight was beyond him, for each movement caused him to moan. So when he wrenched off his blindfold he was still crouched; a wildly grotesque figure with his shaggy hair tangled around his face and his untrimmed beard reaching to the matted hair of his chest.

His weird eyes, glinting with reflected light, looked malevolently around the group of men who had witnessed his humiliation and his punishment. They finally came to rest upon the two men in its center—the Laird and his son. He smeared one hand across his dripping nose and mouth, then said in a voice rasping with hatred:

"Hear me, Sir Alastair! And take this knowledge to bed with you this night. Because of what you have caused that oaf to do to me you have sealed the doom of yourself and your family!"

The words were almost ludicrously melodramatic, yet so arresting was his stance and the palpable radiation of his hatred that everybody in the court-yard fell suddenly silent. The Hermit went on:

"Your family line will become extinct with this son of yours. He shall never have issue to succeed him. The last of the Rathlaws is standing there beside you, Sir Alastair. And so that you shall know that my prediction will come true I will prophesy the omens which will precede its fulfilment."

Sweat cut pale rivulets through the grime on his heaving chest. Compelled into silence, his audience shivered.

"My Laird of Rathlaw, you have a brother. A bachelor. The first omen will come when that brother is struck blind."

Startled eyes turned towards the Laird and his son. Still nobody dared to interrupt the Hermit; the only audible reaction was a rustle of uneasy movement. It was as though he held them all in some evil, hypnotic spell.

"The second omen will be the appearance of a water kelpie from Black Loch." Now the Hermit raised his hands, crooking his splayed fingers in a gesture of utter malevolence. "When that omen is seen, you will know, my Laird of Rathlaw, that your son is soon to die."

And while the audience stood stunned, the Hermit added, with relish:

"And, like your brother who will be struck blind, your son will die without issue. That is my curse and my prophecy."

Grinning, the Hermit glared like a wolf at bay. The Laird himself broke the ensuing silence. He stepped forward and lightly placed an arm around his son's shoulders, smiling his contempt.

"Take him and throw him off my land," he ordered.

There was a brief hesitation before several men converged upon the Hermit and grabbed him. They dragged him towards the Land Rover, and, while he spat obscenities flung him unceremoniously into its back. Another man, carrying a shotgun, got aboard beside the driver and his expression showed that he would be only too glad of a chance to use it if their prisoner gave any further trouble.

As the Land Rover drove out into the darkness and the Hermit's curses faded, Donald crossed to his car and switched off its headlamps. Then he accompanied his father indoors. Within a few moments the

Hermit's prophecy was wiped from their minds like a sponge passing over a slate.

But in the minds of some of the others, as they turned away, the Hermit's words lingered. They remembered the look in the man's eyes, the hate in his voice—and they recalled that in the somber history of the Highlands hate had been known to produce terrifyingly accurate examples of second sight.

Chapter Four

The old house was in an alley off Half Moon Street, London, W.1.

The street reached from Curzon Street at its northern end to Piccadilly, and on the other side of the traffic stream of Piccadilly was the oasis of Green Park.

But the old house was not only in a backwater of Piccadilly; it was also in a backwater of time. Like a withered, senile veteran surviving when all his contemporaries had become casualties of violence or decay, the headquarters of The Guardians was an anachronism—a rickety bridge spanning the gulf of history.

Between two tall soot-stained houses facing Half Moon Street, the alley's narrow entrance suddenly widened into one of the hidden, almost forgotten streets which still persist even in the most expensive parts of Mayfair. This was known as Start Passage and the name was believed to be a derivation of Astarte Passage, named after the Goddess of Love, whose art had been practiced, in earlier days, in the brothels and taverns which stood there.

At Piccadilly less than a hundred yards away. to the south were the Ritz, the Berkeley and the May Fair; also within easy strolling distance were the Dorchester, Grosvenor House and the Hilton. But here the houses were from another era.

They had been erected in what had been open fields at the time when London was being rebuilt after the Great Fire of 1666. Their speculative builders had heeded the words of the Royal Proclamation issued by King Charles on the 13th of September that year that 'no man whatsoever shall presume to erect any house or building, great or small, but of brick or stone.' Throughout the intervening centuries they had been added to, adapted and changed, and round them the great sprawl of London's West End had grown up in steel and concrete.

But Start Passage remained; a silent, secret little street which the years had forgotten. So did the house, although for peace of mind its historical links were better left uninvestigated.

Rumor had it that in this house William Calcraft, public executioner during the reign of Queen Victoria, had once lived—Calcraft, a fumbling, inefficient man who was reputed to have made the business of hanging an unpleasantly protracted affair. This may have explained why he had spent the last few years of his life tended and guarded by other public servants, in an asylum for the incurably insane.

But Calcraft—or his ghost—was not entirely to blame for the uncomfortable aura which the house possessed. Long before he had hanged himself, with characteristic and painful inefficiency, the house in Start Passage had already acquired a disquieting reputation, as if the personalities of previous occupants had adhered in layer upon layer.

The aura came through none of the normal senses. One felt it in the spine, as a chill beginning at waist level and edging its way up between the shoulder-blades. The sensation first prompted visitors to peer nervously behind them—an urge almost instantly obliterated by an infinitely stronger fear of looking behind. One was left with an irresistible impulse to hurry on.

A man taking up permanent residence in this house had to be someone of very exceptional strength of nerve and of very peculiar temperament.

Gideon Cross, present owner and sole permanent occupant, possessed those qualifications in full measure. And the peculiarities of his temperament, like the history of the house itself, were better left uninvestigated. Even his physical appearance, his least peculiar aspect, was arresting.

He was a sparely-built man of medium height, now in his late sixties, with an iron-grey goatee beard and a shock of hair appropriately white. Not so appropriate were his physical fitness and his partiality for attractive young women, who seemed to be his to command.

His personal living quarters were a suite of rooms on the top floor of the old house—a suite which included a vast library, to which no casual visitor had access.

Sir Alastair Rathlaw had no idea even of that library's existence, nor was he interested in any top-floor room when he made his first and last visit to the house.

It was late afternoon when he dismissed the taxi which had brought him from King's Cross railway terminus, after his train journey down from Scotland. He hesitated on the pavement. Behind him the one-way traffic was proceeding normally and prosaically from Piccadilly to Curzon Street. But the house he was facing, though it was one in a row, seemed to stand apart, and Sir Alastair, like others before him, sensed he would be stepping into another age. Yet this was the house in which he had an appointment, and he had already noticed the old-fashioned brass plate confirming the fact. It was fixed to a pillar of the shadowed portico and was engraved in flowing script with only two words: *The Guardians*.

He made a conscious effort and stepped through the portico on to the old worn coconut-fiber mat in the open doorway. Now he was faced with a closed wooden door. A door with about a dozen square panes of glass set into it at chest-level. The glass might as well have been solid wood, since it was dark and opaque.

Already, standing in the little porch, Sir Alastair felt isolated from the normal, everyday world a couple of yards behind him.

But it was on no trifling whim that he had come here. If the help he needed lay on the other side of this door facing him, then the atmosphere of the house did not matter. Nothing inside could be stranger, more somber, than the problem which had brought him from Scotland.

31

His face expressionless, he grasped the old-fashioned metal door-knob and tentatively turned it.

There was no resistance. No resistance, either, to his gentle thrust. With only the very faintest of squeaks from unlubricated hinges, the door swung inwards.

Sir Alastair found himself looking into a small vestibule, at the far end of which could be seen the beginning of a narrow staircase. High up in this staircase, light from an invisible source filtered down, and from its dimness, Sir Alastair guessed that it came from a skylight above the stairwell that was thickly coated with years of London grime.

Again he hesitated, but only briefly. Then he took the decisive step across the threshold into the gloomy hall. Freed of his restraining touch the door swung gently to behind him.

He was in the house of The Guardians.

With the cutting-off of the light from the street, Sir Alastair was plunged into what seemed almost complete darkness. He stood motionless until his eyes adjusted to his surroundings. Something small glimmered half-way up the right-hand wall. It was the yellowed ivory button of a bell-push.

Going towards it, he realized that it was set in a side door until now unnoticed. Beneath the bell-push was a small white card and on this had been typed: 'The Guardians—Reception.'

He pressed the ivory button and the door opened with startling suddenness. The sound of the bell had hardly died away when he found himself looking into the unbanely enquiring face of a very attractive young woman.

She was as tall as himself. Her sleek hair was

raven-black, her eyes brown, and her complexion had a pale purity which was very rare indeed. If her skin had pores, they were imperceptible in its unblemished smoothness. Her lips had a sensual fullness, belied by the cool impersonality of her large eyes. She was, Sir Alastair judged, in her late twenties.

A little awkwardly in the face of her cool composure, he said: "I have an appointment with Mr. Kane—"

"Ah yes," she said briefly. "You must be Sir Alastair Rathlaw."

"That's right."

She stepped back into the room. "Shall I take your hat and coat?"

"Thank you." He moved into the room which he now saw was sparsely furnished as an office. He also saw that the young woman's slim but shapely figure was clad in a black office dress with white collar and cuffs.

As she took his tweed hat and overcoat from him and hung them on a nearby coat-stand, she said:

"We don't employ a receptionist. I'm Anne Ashby, one of the directors. I've been waiting to take you up."

"I see," he murmured vaguely.

It was a strange firm, he thought, in which a director acted as receptionist, though of course a concern of this kind could hardly be expected to have orthodox business methods.

"This way," Anne Ashby invited, indicating the open door.

He moved back into the gloomy hall and instantly found her at his side.

"Mr. Kane is on the first floor," she explained.

As the two of them walked along the hall, Sir Alastair was conscious of a variety of impressions. A faintly musty odor seemed to emanate from the building itself, but was overlaid by a subtle fragrance from the svelte young woman beside him. Underfoot was shiny, slippery linoleum, but beneath this must have been some very old floorboards, because every step caused a faint creaking.

When the Laird and Anne reached the foot of the staircase, Sir Alastair noticed a gap in the wall at his right—the entrance of a narrow passageway leading off to somewhere unknown. But on turning into the stairway and climbing the first couple of steps, he glanced upwards and saw that nothing could be taken for granted here. Light certainly percolated down from above, but not from any skylight. The short, narrow flight led up to a landing, and still none was visible—there remained only diffused illumination from an unknown source.

From the landing, a corridor led to Sir Alastair's left. Straight ahead was another flight of stairs. While the Laird was waiting for directions from his guide, swift footsteps suddenly sounded and from down those stairs appeared the feet and legs of a girl.

Feet, ankles, calves, knees, thighs . . . so much of the thighs appeared that Sir Alastair was beginning to think that the hurrying girl was wearing neither skirt nor dress. The hem of a pale-blue garment then came into view, but Sir Alastair remained embarrassed. Had the wearer been standing on the landing, the mini-dress would have revealed some six inches of thigh. But as she hurried down from above, much more was revealed.

But the Laird need not have blushed. The wearer

34

of the mini-dress, a blonde of nineteen or twenty, approached smiling, as if at some recent happening on the top floor from which she had scampered down, and completely at her ease.

At sight of the Laird and Anne, her expression changed very slightly—not, however, in the direction of self-consciousness. After a flickering glance at Sir Alastair, she gave his escort a smile that was subtly mocking and full of innuendo.

As she brushed past, Anne Ashby returned her smile. But the Laird could see that there was no friendliness between these two young women. Anne's smile conveyed a cool contempt. There was an undercurrent of feeling between them which he could not expect to understand.

When Anne led him into the corridor at his left, Sir Alastair tried to dismiss from his mind everything but the purpose of his visit. But external impressions insisted on intruding. The icily low temperature of this corridor along which he was walking; its heavily oppressive atmosphere. He was not an unduly nervous man, nor had he ever been susceptible to anything that might be regarded as 'psychic influences,' yet he had an eerie awareness of things not perceptible to the eye.

He and his dark-haired escort did not appear to be the only . . . intelligences in this chill corridor. He had the kind of sensation he had known in the past—that somebody was watching him. Only on those past occasions there had been someone human and ordinary watching him, as a glance had confirmed.

Here he saw no one in any direction. Nor did he feel that he was leaving an unseen watcher behind as he walked along the corridor. He had the indefinable feeling that the watcher—or watchers—moved with him. He could not shake off the feeling that he was being accompanied by some form of personality which had watched and waited here for many years.

But a very material knock brought him to the practical present. Anne had tapped on a plain closed door.

A fairly deep, rather pleasant masculine voice inside the room invited: "Come in."

With a twist of the knob Anne flung the door wide open, then stood aside for the visitor to enter first.

Sir Alastair stepped forward on to the soft pile of a thick carpet. Anne's footsteps were inaudible because of the carpet but abruptly the Laird realized that she was again beside him. In a clear, cool voice she said:

"Sir Alastair, please sit down. Mr. Steven Kane is ready to see you. Steven—Sir Alastair Rathlaw."

The Laird stared in bewilderment. He had seated himself in a room that was comfortably furnished, though in an old-fashioned way, with heavy chairs, heavy, dark window curtains, a massive desk in the middle of the room.

But no one was seated behind that desk. Anne Ashby had looked in that direction when announcing the visitor, had spoken as though the 'Steven' she addressed had been sitting or standing there in plain view. As far as Sir Alastair could see, there were only two people in the room—the young woman and himself.

He frowned with resentment. He had come here to have a problem solved, not to be presented with additional ones. Was this man Kane trying to impress

36

him with some foolery involving a microphone. communicating with him from an adjacent room? What was impressive about that? Why take the trouble for such a trifling satisfaction?

Then Sir Alastair gave a start.

Beyond the desk and over near the dark window curtains, at about the height of a fairly tall man, something of lighter tone was materializing. A human ear . . . then the side of a human face. As it turned, like a revolving globe, a man's profile came into view. Continuing to turn, the materializing head could now be seen full-face—a disembodied face gazing straight at Sir Alastair.

Sir Alastair felt a slight superstitious shiver. Then he gave a self-conscious laugh. He realized just what had happened.

There had been no deliberate attempt to impress him. It just so happened that a man had been standing near those dark curtains, with his back to the room. His hair was dark and he was wearing a dark smoking jacket and dark trousers. A black silk scarf, tucked into the smoking jacket, was wound high about his neck, so that with his back turned no flesh had been visible.

In the low-key lighting of the room he had been like a chameleon, its natural camouflage blending with its background so as to produce an illusion of invisibility.

Now the man whose face had 'materialized' from the dark background came towards the desk. Sir Alastair saw that he was tall, sparely but athletically built, with dark hair swept back and dark, penetrating eyes. He was around forty and there was about him an air which immediately inspired the Laird with confidence.

Looking across the desk he said, in the pleasantly deep voice which Sir Alastair had already heard: "I'm Steven Kane. What is your trouble, Sir Alastair?"

The question, coming without preamble, released the Laird's pent-up anxiety like the shattering of a dam. He blurted out:

"My trouble is . . . an omen—or rather, two omens—which have come to warn me."

"To warn you of what, Sir Alastair?"

"That my family is doomed."

And as he spoke the words Sir Alastair looked across at Steven Kane in a desperate appeal which asked him to do the impossible—to prevent the pre-ordained and the inevitable.

To work a miracle.

Chapter Five

Not only to visitors was the house in Start Passage a world away from the familiar backgrounds they had known. Even to Steven Kane, this strange old house was far removed from the academic environment in which he had previously lived.

The only link between his old life and the present was his absorbing, unbroken interest in the Occult.

The investigation of the malign occult in all its many manifestations was the purpose and function of this organization known as The Guardians, of which he was the principal working director. To investigate and do battle with the Powers of Evil was now Kane's chief aim in life.

Even when he had been a professor at Kincaster University, the world-wide and age-old aspects of occultism had been one of his most profound studies. It had, in fact, been this interest which had lost him the Chair of Anthropology and caused his abrupt departure from the academic world. Black magic had proved to be a dangerous subject with which to deal when lecturing a class of skeptical young students.

The next step in Steven Kane's career had been instigated by Gideon Cross, the eccentric and mysterious owner of this house in Start Passage, whose brain-child the organization known as The Guardians had been. At Cross's invitation, soon after the Kincaster University disaster, Kane had assumed control of that organization and launched its operations.

Gideon Cross had remained the *eminence grise* in the top floor suite of rooms, rarely taking any active part. But he did often show a slightly sardonic interest by coming down for an occasional talk with the working directors. And his extensive library of occult lore, in that large room upstairs, was always at their disposal, as was his immense personal knowledge of the paranormal.

One of the other working directors had also been selected and enlisted by Cross himself. This was Anne Ashby. The choice had never ceased to puzzle Kane, for Anne professed a deep dislike for Cross, which was revealed not only in her manner but in her conversation. Yet that dislike did not prevent her from making occasional unexplained and inexplicable visits to his rooms. Once Kane, working long after midnight, had gone up to Cross's rooms to borrow a book; when he had knocked on the door Anne had answered it. She had been dressed in a soft silken wrapper and—Kane was willing to swear—very little else. She had seemed quite unperturbed at the sight of him and as soon as he had entered she had gone into another room and closed the door.

The incident had both puzzled and worried Kane. He knew that a succession of young, nubile girls visited Cross's rooms, but he had not expected to number Anne among that clientele. For one thing, her dislike of Gideon Cross seemed genuine and deep-rooted. But although she claimed not to have known Cross before she joined the organization, Kane had a feeling that she was lying. He sensed an intimacy between them, not so much a physical one as a love-hate relationship to which he could find no satisfactory answer.

His own feelings towards Anne were mixed. She attracted him sexually—as she appeared to attract most men. The movements of her slim body, the graceful turning of her head, her long, dark stare, could send the blood quickening along his veins. Yet at the same time he felt vaguely repelled by her. There was something fey about her—something as faintly sinister perhaps as there was about Gideon Cross himself.

Always at the back of Kane's mind was a discovery he had made in Cross's library upstairs. In one of the old volumes he had come across an item of history which continually provoked him. According to a few paragraphs on a faded page, a woman of West Kent had been indicted at Maidstone Assizes in 1652 on a charge of murder by witchcraft. That woman's name had been Anne Ashby. Her victim, one of Cromwell's Presbyterian colonels, had been named Gideon Cross.

At the trial it had transpired that Colonel Cross, under threats of denouncing the woman Ashby as a witch, had carnally used her; in revenge, she had poisoned him. Those were the facts alleged by the defense.

But according to the prosecution it had been Anne Ashby who had tried to seduce Cross. The woman had been found guilty and hanged, but not before a Maidstone mob had tried to put her to death by fire.

Three present-day facts made this historical item of considerable interest to Kane. First, the living Anne Ashby was an expert on poisons. Second, despite her alleged dislike of Gideon Cross and her claim never to have met him before joining The Guardians, there was undoubtedly an intimacy between them; if not physical, certainly psychical—an intimacy not extended to the other members of Gideon's staff.

Third, Kane was intrigued by Anne's morbid, irrational terror of fire. Even the striking of a match within a few yards of her would cause her to tremble—the only times he could remember seeing her discomposed, for in all other respects she appeared to have nerves of steel.

The paradox of Anne's attitude to Cross, the contradiction between her openly professed dislike of him and her midnight appearance in his room dressed only in the flimsiest of wrappers, made her trustworthiness suspect as far as Kane was concerned —although as yet he had found no reason for mistrust. Unless, perhaps, her intimacy with Cross was in itself something to make him feel uneasy.

On the face of it, such a reason might seem absurd, for it was Gideon Cross himself who had called the organization into being. And yet . . . in the war against malign occultism of any kind and under any label—Black Magic, Satanism, diabolism, the Left Hand Path—one had to be on guard against the most subtle of strategies.

Even in military warfare, Kane reasoned, the most dangerous enemy was the unsuspected enemy within one's own ranks, the fifth-columnist in one's own uniform. Similarly, the most effective and dangerous agent of the malign powers would be one ostensibly working for the opposition.

It was merely a thought, scarcely a suspicion even, prompted by the odd facets of Gideon's enigmatic personality and of the organization he had created. It was probably an unjust thought. But it had occurred to Steven Kane on more than one occasion that, working together in this organization and operating from this headquarters, he and his other co-directors—Lionel Marks and the Reverend John Dyball—could more easily be kept under surveillance than they could have been as unconnected fighters against the forces of evil.

Always Steven Kane's plans, decisions and assumptions had to be hedged about with mental reservations. Always he had metaphorically to watch his back in case of a stab from a direction which should have been above suspicion. Gideon Cross and Anne Ashby . . . were they in truth his friends and fellow workers, or his secret enemies?

But none of these mental reservations regarding his colleagues could have been guessed from the calmly intent expression on his face as he turned to greet Sir Alastair Rathlaw.

He said: "Two omens—to warn you that your family is doomed. Tell me about it, Sir Alastair."

Anne Ashby had closed the door and moved unobtrusively across the carpet to stand beside the desk, her long-lashed eyes fixed steadily upon the Laird. As always, even when his interest was elsewhere, Steven Kane was conscious of her presence.

Without removing his own gaze from Kane's face, Sir Alastair said hesitantly: "To begin at the beginning, I must tell you about something which happened at the Castle just on a year ago . . ." He went on to relate the events of that night when Fergus Trayle, the Hermit of Black Loch, had been brought to him for judgment after his assault on Jean Patterson.

"I had the man flogged, Mr. Kane. I gave the task of flogging him to the young fellow the girl was engaged to—and I must admit he made a good job of it. When it was over the Hermit—he was practically foaming at the mouth with fury as well as with pain—called down a curse on myself and my son, Donald. He said that my family would become extinct with Donald, who would never have issue. And so that I would know that the prediction would come true, he prophesied two omens which would precede it."

Anne's pale face leaned forward over the desk; her eyes were intent. "And they were?" she asked quietly.

The Laird said bleakly: "I have a brother, Malcolm, a bachelor, younger than myself by a few years. Trayle said that the first omen would come when Malcolm was struck blind. The second omen would be the appearance of a water kelpie from Black Loch—"

"A water kelpie being a young horse, according to the old superstition," nodded Kane. "In the occult lore of your Scottish highlands, Sir Alastair, the East Coast kelpie is golden or yellow and never changes its form, but the West Coast kelpie is either brown or black and is traditionally capable of assuming human form. Do you agree?"

Sir Alastair gave a brief, mirthless smile. "I see you know your subject, Mr. Kane. Until recently I was extremely skeptical about folklore and superstitions—even when Trayle hurled his curses at me I thought nothing of it."

Kane saw the Laird's forehead crease into lines of worry and he said, sympathetically: "But since then something has happened which made you change your mind?"

The Laird nodded. In a slow, hesitant voice he said, "A month ago I was playing a round of golf with Malcolm on my private links near the Castle. There was but a single cloud in the sky—a large, heavy cloud moving slowly and bringing no rain; we scarcely noticed it. Like myself, Malcolm was using steel-shafted clubs. He was just swinging for a long drive, when there was a flash of lightning which flashed directly from that black cloud. Malcolm was knocked unconscious and when he recovered, he was blind. Completely blind." His hands closed upon the arms of his chair, so tightly that the white bone of his knuckles showed against the brown skin.

"And . . . . ?" Kane's voice was quiet but inflexible. He did not question Sir Alastair's statement concerning that ominous black cloud or the malevolent force which had issued from it. He knew that there were dark powers abroad throughout the world against which all humanity, if it was to survive, had to be constantly on guard. His task was to fight them and, if possible, overthrow and destroy them; to that end he was here.

"His sight has never returned," went on the Laird. "And last week, two of the girls on my domestic staff were late getting back from an evening out with their boy friends. They gave a strange excuse. They said they had been to Black Loch, where the Hermit had once lived—"

Kane said sharply: "*Once* lived? When did he leave?"

"Oh, soon after the flogging. That old shack of his has been empty for nearly a year now. Otherwise nothing would have got those young people within miles of it."

Anne said, her dark, glowing eyes still fixed inscrutably on the Laird's face: "So they went down to the Loch—and they saw a water kelpie."

The Laird, startled, said: "That's right—you've guessed it, Miss Ashby. They were excited and a little nervous, but they swore that what they saw was *not* imagination. After all, it would be difficult for four people to imagine the same thing."

"Not necessarily," said Kane, "if hypnosis was involved. But go on, Sir Alastair. Tell me what the two girls saw—"

"They saw a yellow horse come trotting along from the direction of the Loch, and disappear into the woods. All four of them noticed that it was streaming wet and that its hooves made no sound."

Kane gave the Laird a penetrating stare. "You don't think the two young couples cooked up this story as an excuse for the girls being late?"

"Why should they? They could have easily concocted some other more plausible story—such as getting trapped by the mist or staying too long in the village. They're rather simple girls, Mr. Kane—too simple to have deliberately lied about what they saw, or thought they saw."

Kane's long, strong fingers tapped lightly on the desk top for a second, then he said: "What happened then?"

"Nothing. They hid for a while, frightened that the kelpie would return—frightened perhaps that the Hermit himself might be lurking there. If their story had been the only . . . omen, I probably wouldn't have thought twice about it. But coupled with Malcolm's blindness—"

"Quite," nodded Kane. "That tragic event naturally predisposed you to accept their story. Well, let's give them the benefit of the doubt and accept the fact that they did see something resembling a water kelpie. Does anyone in that particular part of the world own a palomino? A pony of that color—fawn, with a white mane and tail—might reasonably suggest a golden kelpie to four imaginative young people steeped in the folklore of the Highlands. Particularly since it appeared near the Loch."

Sir Alastair frowned and shook his head. "I've never heard of anyone in the neighborhood owning a palomino. In any case, the animal was wet—as though it had just come out of the Loch. No real horse would have gone into the Loch—or if it had, it would have been a ten-to-one chance of its coming out alive. They say the Loch is bottomless. And the other thing—about its hooves making no sound as it moved. In fact, one of the girls stated that it seemed to be pacing *above* the ground—two or three inches above it—"

Kane swung his chair around and stared out of the window; against the light his profile showed almost hawk-like, the features strong and pronounced. Then he turned back and said quietly:

"I think you are being unduly concerned, Sir Alastair. It would be foolish to base your fears upon the statement of four rather credible youngsters—"

"But Malcolm's blindness!" protested the Laird. "The Hermit predicted it—he predicted that he would be *struck blind*. And he was. That was genuine enough."

Kane nodded. "Yes. And in itself much more important than the alleged water kelpie, of course. But as an omen, the blinding of your brother was less important. Until the second omen came to pass you would have nothing to fear."

"But when it did," the Laird exclaimed agitatedly, "it would be a sign that Donald would die. That is why I came to see you—not only for your advice, but for your help."

Kane got suddenly to his feet and began to pace the dimly-lighted room. In all his movements there was a forcefulness which oddly impressed the Laird. Here was a man not only of intelligence, but of action; a man who would use his physical strength, if need be, as swiftly and unquestioningly as he would use the powers of his mind. In spite of his distress, Sir Alastair began to feel vaguely reassured.

"Everything," Kane said ruminatively, "seems to

depend on the genuineness of this alleged water kelpie. If it wasn't a genuine kelpie, then you have no reason to fear for your son until a genuine water kelpie *does* appear."

"But it has—"

"Not to you or your son—or to anybody in whose veracity you could have complete confidence," Kane pointed out. "It merely 'appeared' to four rather impressionable young people. They saw a pony—and the mist and moonlight, coupled with their own imagination—turned it into a water kelpie. As for the blinding of your brother, however deeply unfortunate that was, it cannot necessarily be counted as an omen. The faculty of precognition is a proven fact of parapsychology. The Hermit may well have foreseen the accident, and even the story told by those young people about the water kelpie. It wouldn't be the first time there had been stories about this fabled animal, I gather?"

Relief showed faintly in Sir Alastair's face. "No. The Highlands abound with such superstitions, of course."

Kane stopped and leaned forward, looking like an eagle about to swoop upon its prey. "Don't you see, Sir Alastair, if the Hermit foresaw your brother's accident—and it may well be that he has second sight, not an uncommon phenomenon even outside Scotland—and knew that sooner or later somebody would revive the story of having seen a water-kelpie, he could have pretended that they foretold your son's death? In his state of mind, where hate and malice were obviously the foremost emotions, he might well do such a thing, knowing that when they came to pass you would be desperately worried."

"But if he foresaw my son's death—"

Kane said shrewdly: "So far we have only his word for it that he did. In fact, the only thing that we have absolute proof he *did* foresee was the blinding of your brother, Malcolm."

Sir Alastair pursed his lips dubiously. "But if he could foresee Malcolm's accident, why should he not have foreseen something happening to Donald?"

"Even genuine clairvoyants with no malicious motives sometimes make mistakes—or enlarge on what they actually see. And from the Hermit's viewpoint, two omens would be much more impressive than one." Kane looked at the Laird gravely. "I'm going to be quite frank with you, Sir Alastair. I mentioned the possibility that he could have foreseen your brother's blindness, which was a physical thing. But his omen regarding the appearance of the water kelpie inclines most definitely towards the supernatural—or to some form of trickery. And if trickery *was* involved; perhaps some form of hypnosis, if the Hermit was still hiding somewhere near the Loch, there is the possibility that he *intends* to make his third prediction come true. That during the time between the blinding of your brother and the manifestation of this so-called kelpie, he has conceived a plan to avenge himself upon your son—"

The Laird paled. "You mean . . . kill him? By God, if he should dare to lay a single hand upon Donald—"

Kane began to strip off his silk scarf and smoking jacket. No longer looking at the Laird he said:

"If the Hermit genuinely foresaw your son's death, and it is to come from natural causes, there is nothing I can do but recommend a complete medical check-up for him. But if the Hermit invented that prediction with the intention of making it come true—"

He turned and spoke crisply to Anne Ashby.

"Anne—would you phone Lionel? I've an idea we shall be needing some very private inquiries concerning our friend the Hermit."

Chapter Six

Lionel Marks climbed out of his hired Land Rover and plodded wearily but purposefully up to the ramshackle gate of the tiny croft. After opening the gate and passing through he carefully re-closed it behind him and made his way along the path to the equally ramshackle little farmhouse.

Legwork was no novelty to Lionel Marks, ex-private detective. But this was the seventh croft he had visited this afternoon. His feet, accustomed to the evenness of city streets and still in thin-soled city shoes, were hot and tired from the strain of walking over rugged and stony country.

Although it was early evening, Marks was feeling warm from his exertions, so he had left his hat in the Land Rover. His sparse hair was ruffled by a slight breeze, but temperamentally Marks was completely unruffled. Much of his career had consisted of prolonged and unfruitful legwork of a routine nature. The only difference being that today he was doing it in the wide open spaces.

Marks was a Jew, though not an orthodox one. His plump, easy-going appearance belied the sharpness of the mind behind the twinkling black eyes and the fact that he was not only tough but could be ruthless. He was in his early forties, married, with a teenage daughter whom he openly worshipped. He was extremely garrulous and at times even excitable, and he had a keen sense of humor which was sometimes spiced with malice. Also he possessed a fund of funny and often scurrilous stories about his life as a 'private eye.'

The little croft he was now approaching was privately owned, the property of the crofter. It was situated near the boundary of the Rathlaw estate, not far from the Black Glen and Black Loch.

Marks's inquiries had been made both on the Laird's estate and outside it. He had been trying to find out if anyone possessed a palomino pony, or if anyone knew of one in the vicinity. That type of question had seemed more practical than than asking about a yellow kelpie.

But even with this question he had drawn a blank, until inquiring at the sixth croft on his list. The family living there had recommended him to try his luck at the farmhouse he was now approaching —the domain of Aggie and Jamie Erskine.

"If it's ponies ye want tae lairn aboot," the crofter had said, "then it's the Erskines ye need tae see. Jamie Erskine has the Horseman's Word."

Marks knew that in the Highlands, 'word' had several cabalistic connotations. It could mean a spell or a curse. The Horseman's Word was specific, a traditional spell applying only to equine animals.

According to Highland folklore there had from early times been a Brotherhood of the Horseman's Word, with its own secret rites. Initiation of new members had always taken place—and was said still to take place today—in a farrier's smithy, with the blacksmith acting as High Priest. Initiates knew a spell which would instantly tame the wildest of horses.

The information that someone living so near Black Loch had the legendary Horseman's Word had brought a faint smile to Marks's smooth face. It was the day's first hint of anything with a possible bearing on the recent report of a water-kelpie emerging from Black Loch.

He had been given no further information even by the family on the sixth croft. Nothing to give him any idea of what Aggie and Jamie Erskine looked like. But he was expecting another weather-beaten, hard-working married couple similar to those crofters he had already met.

So the actuality came as a surprise.

He crunched up the last yard of the stony path and came to a halt at the closed door. He had already deduced, from the weeds flanking the path, that the Erskines were not quite as hard-working as the other crofters in the neighborhood. The cracked front door confirmed that impression, because evidently no attempt had been made to repair it.

No door-knocker was visible, so he rapped with his knuckles. There was no reply; no sign of life.

He knocked again, louder.

The door did not open. But movement at a window a yard away caught his sharp eye. He saw someone peering out at him between the curtains. It was a woman and as she caught his gaze she gave him a sudden wide grin.

Oddly, that grin did nothing to make Lionel Marks feel pleased. The life of Highland crofters was too hard for most of them to give ready signs of pleasure. Few of those he had called on that day had greeted him with even a smile. But as the woman's face was withdrawn, Marks decided to await her at the door with a blandly conventional smile of his own.

At last a chain rattled on the other side of the door. Then it slowly opened to the extent of about ten inches.

Through the gap Marks saw that the still grinning woman was fairly tall with a face bearing traces of a faded beauty. But even from the little he could see of her clothing and hair it was obvious that whatever she had been, she was now little more than a slut.

True, few crofter's wives had the facilities for giving themselves elegant coiffeurs. But this woman —presumably Aggie Erskine—had merely dragged her hair tightly back over her head and tied a piece of old string around it. Leaving the ends, Marks noted sardonically, hanging in a 'pony-tail.'

A button was missing from the front of her frayed blouse, and a tuft of the original thread still projected. There the blouse gaped to reveal a wrinkled, ill-fitting old camisole. A flickering glance told him that beneath the frayed hem of the long skirt she wore, the woman's ankles were bare. On her feet were men's carpet slippers, through which the untrimmed nails of her two big toes protruded.

It was fairly obvious that in this sluttish state the woman would look older than she actually was.

Marks judged her to be no more than thirty-five years old. He also judged that her husband, Jamie, was not a fastidious man if he could tolerate such squalor in the person of his spouse.

But squalor wasn't the only unusual aspect of her appearance. Her pale eyes, unblinking and wide open, regarded him with an expression which made Marks feel vaguely uncomfortable. Her grinning mouth was slightly open, to reveal the tip of her tongue.

Marks broke the heavy silence. "Mrs. Erskine?" he asked politely.

She gave a girlish giggle as though he had made the funniest remark of the century. And she ogled him, quite unmistakably.

Lionel Marks would perhaps have been the first to admit that, in appearance, he was unlikely to set feminine hearts a-flutter. Neither his near-rotundity, his incipient baldness, nor the smallness of the boot-button eyes beneath their overhanging brows were, he considered, calculated to inspire love at first sight. Consequently he was more than a little taken aback at the woman's undoubted overture.

He was mentally adjusting himself to the peculiarity of the situation when a face suddenly appeared beside the woman. A masculine face.

But it was not the face of her husband. It appeared at waist level, peeping around the woman's hip. It was the small face of a boy of about ten years old—presumably her son.

Marks liked youngsters. His smile broadened and he said in an almost avuncular way: "Hello, sonny—"

The woman said, still grinning: "I'm not married." She gave another giggle of irrepressible mirth. Then, cheerfully, she went on: "Jamie's ma bairn. But he's a bastard."

Marks blinked. He had prided himself on the fact that his varied and somewhat checkered career had made him virtually shock-proof. He had flattered himself that there was no personality-type that he had not, at some time, met. But Aggie Erskine was quite a discovery.

So was Jamie.

Because, Marks reasoned, if Aggie had no husband this ten-year-old boy must be the Jamie who had the Horseman's Word. And somehow he did not look old enough to have been initiated into an occult Brotherhood by a brawny blacksmith.

If he did have the legendary Horseman's Word, where had he learned it?

For a moment even Marks's ready tongue was at a loss. Then he asked: "This boy, your son, is he the *only* Jamie Erskine hereabouts?"

"Och!" she answered. "Sure he is. I telt ye I've nae husband—"

Which fact, Marks reflected wryly, had obviously not prevented her from producing Jamie.

He shifted from one foot to the other, not quite sure how to proceed. From her perpetual grin he was rapidly getting the impression that it would be futile to expect rational conversation from her.

He was also becoming increasingly aware of something very strange in the way young Jamie was staring at him. From under the untrimmed, uncombed fringe of his tow-like hair, the boy's round eyes were gazing curiously at him—not with childish inquisitiveness, however, but with a kind of mocking comprehension. The mind behind that face, thought Marks shrewdly, was a great deal older than the face itself.

Once more Marks turned his genial smile upon the boy. "So you're Jamie?" he said.

The boy opened his mouth slightly, but only a hiss came from between his lips. With undiminished cheerfulness his mother explained: "He cannae talk. He's mute."

Marks felt a pang of genuine pity go through him. He was always affected by the physically handicapped, especially where children were concerned. Perhaps more especially in view of the bouncing good health and complete normality of his daughter, Myra.

He said sympathetically: "He can hear?"

"Och, aye! As well as yersel'."

"I'm glad to meet you then, Jamie," said Marks, infusing a note of heartiness into the words. But even as he spoke he was not quite sure that he meant them. Marks's nerves were strong, but there was something peculiarly nerve-racking about this small boy with his coolly observant eyes and his silent tongue.

To the woman he said: "May I talk with you—" He was about to add 'Mrs. Erskine,' but something stopped him. It may have been her sardonic expression. And as he could hardly address her as 'Miss' Erskine with her offspring standing beside her, Marks decided to dispense with the formality altogether.

The woman stepped aside. "Aye, come in," she invited.

The boy slipped away from her as she swung the door open and Marks's fastidious nostrils distended as he entered the little farmhouse. He walked into a room

56

which looked like the proverbial chinashop through which a bull had recently rampaged. A room almost audibly crying out for the use of a vacuum cleaner, or even for a broom.

Although it was evening and the curtains were drawn, the room was unlit. There were no electric light fixtures. Yet in the gloom Marks saw something on the cluttered floor that stopped him in his tracks.

It was a pony's bridle.

He turned quickly to the woman, the blandness wiped from his face as though a sponge had been passed over it. "You've a pony here?" he asked.

"Pony?" The woman stared at him, still with that inane—or insane—grin. Then she gave another giggle. "A pony, forbye! We cudnae afford a wee duggie—I cudnae feed even a cat!"

Marks judged from the obvious presence of mice —and possibly some even larger rodent—in the house, the cat could well have fed itself. He gestured towards the bridle.

"But the bridle—"

Possibly the boy was a lip-reader, for suddenly he ran out of the room and Marks heard water running. A minute later he returned, carrying a galvanized bucket.

With one foot he cleared a space on the floor and set the bucket down. Marks saw that it was half-full of water.

The boy glanced quickly around him, snatched up the bridle and waved it over the bucket. As he did so he turned to stare at Marks with evident invitation, waving his hand in the direction of the water.

Marks went forward, slowly. With the bridle hanging from his hand Jamie gazed into the bucket and gave a strange smile which sent a cold shiver up Marks's spine—and Marks was not given to cold shivers.

He leaned over to peer into the bucket. Its interior was in shadow and the surface of the water was dark. But Marks saw on that dark surface a human face.

At first he thought it was his own reflection. Then he realized that the hair of the head was long and shaggy, the beard untrimmed, and that the eyes were glaring up at him malevolently. For a moment Marks felt the back of his neck prickle, but he overcame the sensation and leaned further over the bucket. As he did so the entire face vanished.

Marks closed his eyes and opened them again. Had he imagined that baleful, bearded countenance?

As he straightened up, there came a sound which momentarily transfixed him with its unexpectedness. It was a shrill, piercing whistle which seemed to screech through his ear-drums and echo like the yowling of bag-pipes through his head. He whirled round. The sound had come from Jamie.

The boy had dropped the bridle and was staring across at the closed door. There was something almost terrifying in his tense expectancy.

Involuntarily Marks gazed in the same direction; behind him he was conscious of the nearness of the woman and from the corner of his eye he saw that her grin was now knowing and eager.

The waiting was very short.

Suddenly, Marks heard new sounds—the thudding sounds of a horse's hoofs, coming nearer and nearer. There was a gusty panting at close range, followed by an excited whinny just outside the door and a pawing sound on the path. The panting became so loud that Marks judged the animal must be right on the doorstep.

With a violent effort he shook off the peculiar inertia which seemed to be holding him and leaped towards the door. He grabbed at the handle and yanked it open. Outside it was dusk, but after the gloom inside the farmhouse, he could see quite clearly.

And the path leading to the door was empty.

"By the Lord Harry—!" Marks took a few puzzled steps forward, staring around him. There was utterly no sign of life at all, either animal or human. Nothing to obstruct his view of the path from doorway to distant gate.

He could not believe it. He ran out of the house and along the path, looking in all directions. Nothing. Yet the animal which had made so much noise galloping towards the house could not have galloped away in silence, in spite of the fact that the pawing and panting had stopped the instant Marks had opened the door.

Marks ran right down to the gate. Not even at full gallop could a horse have got out of sight in such a short time. Where, in the name of sanity, was it?

The empty landscape mocked him.

Turning, Marks walked slowly back to the house. The front door was still wide open and Aggie and Jamie Erskine were just inside the doorway, looking at him. And now it was not only the woman who had a wide, fixed grin on her face.

Jamie too was grinning, and as he surveyed Marks knowingly, he was literally hugging himself with malicious glee.

When Marks returned to Rathlaw Castle, where he and Steven Kane were staying, he went straight to the room which had been allotted to his co-director, and he entered without even the formality of a knock. Within five minutes he had spilled out the whole story.

"What did you do after that?" Kane asked. In spite of himself he could not help but feel faintly amused. It was the first time he remembered seeing the normally down-to-earth agent so obviously disconcerted.

Marks snorted. "What the hell d' you think I did? Came away, of course. It was useless to ask the woman any questions—she was a nut-case if ever I saw one. And the boy couldn't talk. I still can't make up my mind whether he played a practical joke on me or whether he really did conjure up some diabolical picture in that bucket of his!" He added, reflectively: "By my life, I'd like to know who his father is—or was!"

"Maybe it was his father you saw in the bucket," said Kane gravely.

"If it was, then I saw the Devil," said Marks. He sat down on the edge of Kane's bed and felt in his pocket for his cigarette case. He went on: "It wasn't the actual hocus-pocus—if you can call it that—which upset me, but the involvement of the boy. This kind of thing always seems more diabolical if children are involved."

Kane said: "Your description of that face has a strong resemblance to the Laird's description of the Hermit. Do you think perhaps your experience was due to—shall I say—an association of ideas?"

"No!" snapped Marks, and now there was an edge in his voice. "You know me, Steven—I'm not the imaginative type. What I saw in that damn bucket I really saw. Then there's the bridle; there was no fakery about that, at least. To me it proves that

60

there *is* a pony somewhere on that farm, though it beats me how it was spirited away from that front door!"

Kane was silent a moment, rubbing his hand roughly around the angle of his jaw—a habit he had when he was deeply perplexed. Then he said: "You know, of course, that in the occult lore of the Highlands there are legends of a magic bridle used to conjure up apparitions in a pail of water. One Scots family is said to possess such a bridle still—originally obtained from a water kelpie."

Marks raised one of his thick eyebrows in a quizzical gesture. "So you think that what I heard might not have been a real horse, but a water-kelpie?"

"I'm saying it's possible," said Kane cautiously. "The whistle Jamie gave was probably his version of the Horseman's Word—perhaps the only sound he can make. But it seems he knew just what you'd come about. He showed you not only a vision of his father—who may be Fergus Trayle—but also summoned up the kelpie."

"But how did he know?" demanded Marks. "The only question I got a chance to ask was whether they had a pony on the farm." Then an expression of slow surprise crossed his plump features and he looked at Kane sharply. "Are you suggesting that he might have . . . hypnotized me into seeing that face—and hearing the horse gallop to the front door?"

"It's a possibility," replied Kane. "They say the Hermit has hypnotic powers. If Jamie *is* his natural son, it might well be that he's inherited some of them—"

"Pshaw!" said Marks and grinned. "A man of my superior intellect being hypnotized by a ten-year-old boy! Impossible. Though mind you," he added, "I'm not saying it hasn't been tried—that daughter of mine will go to any lengths to get her own way. Incidentally, it's her birthday next week—"

Kane's dark eyes flickered with amusement. "Is that so? I must remember to get her something. What do teenage girls like most?"

"Teenage boys," said Marks promptly. Then his face sobered. "But to get back to our water-kelpie; however it was done, it indicates one thing—a complete sense of security. That little devil was openly laughing at me, challenging me to make what I could of it all and knowing all the time that whatever conclusion I came to, there was nothing I could do about it. The woman may not know anything—though I'm not so sure that stupid grin wasn't part of the whole masquerade—but, by Harry, the boy knows a sight too much!"

"Still," said Kane equably, "your visit wasn't wasted. If Jamie can conjure up an audible kelpie, he can presumably conjure up a visible one—"

"Or hypnotize people into thinking they see one? Like those two young couples?"

"Exactly. Either way the effect is the same. But there's a very strong inference that both the Erskine woman and her son know Fergus Trayle—"

Marks sniffed. "If Jamie is Fergus's son, then I'd say she knows him very well indeed. No accounting for tastes, of course—by the Lord Harry, Steven, you should have seen her! She looked like something out of Macbeth."

"Judging from reports, the Hermit isn't particularly attractive himself," remarked Kane. Then he went on: "If the Hermit is still in the district—but lying low for reasons of his own—he could well be making use of the boy. The vital thing is to find him before anything happens."

"To Donald Rathlaw, you mean?" asked Marks and now his expression was deadly serious. He leaned forward and stubbed out his cigarette in the tray on Kane's bedside table before adding: "You really believe he's in danger, Steven?"

"It's possible—more than possible, in fact. And if danger is coming, we've got to know from what direction."

"True enough," concurred Marks. "But just how do we find Fergus Trayle?"

Kane raised his dark eyebrows. "By occult means, of course," he said softly. "How else?"

Chapter Seven

The occult means which Steven Kane employed for the purpose of locating Fergus Trayle consisted of a series of experiments involving some very commonplace objects. A pen, a number of maps, a gold ring and a length of string. Also an empty matchbox.

The experiments took place in Kane's room in Rathlaw Castle, almost immediately following his conversation with Marks.

The gold ring was suspended at the lower end of the length of string so that together they formed a pendulum.

This was not the first time that Kane had made use of this simple apparatus. But it was not apparatus with which anyone could get results. These depended on an unexplained faculty possessed by the person using it.

In the course of his researches into the many branches of occultism, Steven Kane had discovered that he was a natural 'dowser.' The familiar dowser was the gifted person who could find buried minerals of water by means of a twig which, in that person's hands, would twitch when passing over the substance being sought.

A more refined kind of dowsing was that practiced with the use of a pendulum and this was known as radiesthesia. It was more refined because it was less limited in its scope, more subtle in its distinctions.

In the hands of a person gifted as a radiesthetist, it would indicate not only the location of lost objects and persons, but even the sex of animals and people. Held over a pregnant woman, it would indicate the sex of her unborn child. Held over a portrait, it would indicate the sex of the person in the photograph.

Lionel Marks had on many occasions witnessed Steven Kane's gift as a radiesthetist put to practical use. But the sight had never lost its fascination for him. So he watched intently when Kane spread on his bed a large-scale map of the Rathlaw estate and its immediate vicinity.

Kane's purpose was to discover the present location of Fergus Trayle. But to do that by means of radiesthesia he needed something which had been in contact with the Hermit and which could transmit his personal vibrations.

To obtain such an object had not been difficult. Together Kane and Marks had gone to Trayle's old bothy, where they had found a number of things he had left behind when he had abandoned his home so hurriedly.

Most retained an odor which had made Kane very reluctant to handle them. Sweaty socks, tattered underclothes, a frayed handkerchief—Kane had been relieved when Marks's sharp eyes had spotted an empty matchbox. At least it did not stink.

Now Kane held the matchbox in his left hand, together with his own pen as a pointer. With his right hand he held the pendulum. Methodically he 'quartered' the map, watching the pendulum for reactions.

Marks's breathing was clearly audible in the quiet room. The agent frankly admitted that where things occult were concerned he was, in comparison with Kane and the other Guardians, a mere initiate. His investigations usually took him along much more material paths; consequently he tended to look upon Kane's psychical activities with an admiring and at times somewhat awed eye.

Presently Kane said: "Negative. That means he's no longer in the neighborhood. We'll have to go further afield, I'm afraid. Open that small-scale map of Scotland, will you, Lionel?"

Marks did so and watched even more closely as Kane repeated the experiment.

Over the northern area of the second map there was again no response. But as Kane moved his pointer southwards, the pendulum's clockwise oscillation suddenly reversed.

This happened first when Kane was pointing the pen in his left hand towards Stirlingshire. The gyration became faster and extended to a larger circle when Kane moved the pointer southwest in the direction of Glasgow.

He continued the movement of the pointer southwards beyond Glasgow. Then the gyration diminished in speed and extent. By a series of trials he found that the response was at its maximum directly above the city itself.

Marks's nose was almost touching the map; he looked up triumphantly. "The Clyde area!" he exclaimed. "But Glasgow's still Britain's third largest city. Where the hell are we going to find him in a place that size?"

Kane grinned. "To get more precise information we'll need a large-scale plan of Glasgow. There's one among that batch of maps I brought up from my car. Dig it out, will you?"

Marks rummaged through the collection of maps on the bedside table and found the one required. Again the experiment was repeated. And when the result had been tested six times over the plan of the city, Kane looked at Marks with a grunt of satisfaction.

"At this moment," he said, with the slight air of pedantry which he sometimes affected and which irritated Marks for some reason he could never wholly explain, "Fergus Trayle is somewhere in Glasgow's Kelvinside district. I get a strong response over any part of that district, so it isn't possible to pinpoint the precise street he's in. That may not matter, anyway —for all we know he may simply be traveling through Kelvinside on the way to where he is actually living."

"We should worry," said Marks. "Once there we

should be able to smell him out—literally." Then, glancing up into Kane's serious face, he added: "What do we do, Steven?"

"Try again later to see if the reaction still comes over Kelvinside. I'll give it a couple of hours—meanwhile, I'll ask the Laird if he has a Glasgow directory."

"Why?"

Kane smiled. "For all we know that shack Trayle lived in may have been only one of his places of . . . residence. It's not impossible he has a home somewhere in Glasgow."

Marks grimaced. "If he had a house or flat in Kelvinside smelling like that shack of his near Black Loch, he'd have the sanitary inspector on his track," he said.

"You've got smells on the brain," said Kane. "Let's be charitable and allow for the possibility that it's only in the country he allows himself to get filthy. Certainly he couldn't move about in public in a place like Glasgow in the condition the Laird described."

"Who says not?" asked Marks. "They've got their share of beatniks too in Glasgow. Long hair, beards, the lot." Then, reverting to Kane's previous remark, he said: "You think he may have had a house in Glasgow long enough for it to be listed in the city directory?"

"It's a possibility. No point in excluding it without first testing, is there?"

Kane discovered that the Laird did in fact possess a current directory of Glasgow. He brought the book back to his room and he and Marks stood shoulder to shoulder as Kane turned the pages. A few minutes later Kane turned to meet Marks's glance.

"There's a Trayle living in Kelvinside," he summarized, "but not a Fergus Trayle. A Mr. Cosmo Trayle."

Marks's face showed disappointment. "Then he can't be our man. If he wanted to hide his identity he'd use a false surname, too."

Kane nodded agreement. "True. We can take it that he isn't living in Glasgow under the name of Cosmo Trayle. But it's quite likely that this Cosmo is a relative of his, and Fergus could be staying with him—"

"There's a long, long Trayle a-winding . . ." murmured Marks, then broke off to dodge an imaginary blow. "Sorry. That one was pretty awful."

"It was damn awful," said Kane. "If you can't do any better than that, for God's sake keep quiet. Anyway, to go back to friend Fergus—there's an obvious way of testing the possibility I mentioned. If we get the same reaction to the pendulum in an hour or two from now, we'll be taking a trip to Glasgow."

Then he frowned. "If Fergus Trayle really does intend to bring about Donald's death—and that's the assumption we're working on—I wonder what means he plans to use. Murder by physical violence or black magic?"

Marks said: "If he intends to stay in Glasgow it'll have to be either murder by magic or by proxy. Donald has no intention of going to Glasgow, has he?"

"No—at least, not that I'm aware of. But we can't rule out your suggestion, Lionel—that of murder by proxy. He might consider it too dangerous to return here; and certainly the moment he's spotted the Laird and everyone else will be on their guard. So it might well be that he would prefer to use an agent—which would establish an alibi for himself at the same time."

"True," said Marks. "We don't know how long he's been in Glasgow, or what resources he has there —human or paranormal. In fact, we know very little about him really, only what the Laird has been able to tell us. But even from that, and from what I saw and heard at the Erskine croft, I've an idea that —if the Hermit really is planning to kill young Donald —he'll do it in his own peculiar way. And the sooner we learn more about him and his peculiar ways, the better."

"Let's hope," said Kane, a trifle sententiously, "that Mr Cosmo Trayle will give us a lead to do just that."

Two hours later Steven Kane, in his Jaguar, and Lionel Marks in his MG convertible, left Rathlaw Castle for the city of Glasgow.

Cosmo Trayle, of the Kelvinside district of Glasgow, Scotland's largest city, was a man who made almost a fetish of cleanliness. By his closest acquaintances—though even they could not claim to be real intimates of his—this extreme concern about personal cleanliness was regarded as a reaction against the shaggy unkemptness of his brother Fergus.

Except in four respects there could hardly have been two brothers more dissimilar to each other than Fergus and Cosmo Trayle.

They were similar in physique. They both had weirdly unmatched eyes. Both were practitioners of the paranormal. And both were practitioners of merciless wickedness.

But even in the respective ways in which they approached the paranormal they differed. Fergus was fundamentally a man of remote places, drawing his inspiration and power from the occult lore of pre-industrial centuries. Cosmo, publicly at least, was a man of the twentieth century, cultured and sophisticated in temperament, domestic background and dress.

He practiced openly—and for huge fees—psychometry, art of gathering, from physical contact with an article, impressions relating to the person with whom it had been most in contact.

The psychometrist's extra-sensory impressions could be both clairvoyant and clairaudient, that is, psychically visible or audible. Also, they could cause the practitioner to feel any pain suffered by the previous possessor of the article. And they could concern that person's past, present or future.

Cosmo Trayle had no need to advertise in the magazines catering for people interested in precognition. Word-of-mouth recommendations brought him even more clients than he had time available. For some of his clients remained attached to him permanently—or for as long as they lived.

Cosmo Trayle did not divulge the grounds on which he chose these favored few. Whether it was because of their special, unlimited interest in the occult, or because of what he discerned of their material circumstances, they were invited to join his Psychic Development Circle.

These initiates soon came to regard the money they possessed as dross compared to the world's need of enlightenment about the Other Side. Willingly, they contributed large sums to the cause of psychic development—the cause as represented by Cosmo Trayle. So all, both the living contributors and those who in their wills bequeathed their all to Cosmo

Trayle, were in effect innocent sheep among wolves.

But not only the wealthy had Cosmo Trayle taken into his Psychic Development Circle. There had been clients with qualifications which to him were almost as attractive as money—qualities of depravity and ruthlessness which had equally appealed as 'suitable.' And whereas the innocents made little progress in psychic development, those chosen for the other reason added rapidly to their depravity under his expert tuition. And their depravity added to Cosmo's power.

In Cosmo Trayle both motives, the love of money and the lust for power, existed behind the suave, elegant facade which so impressed visitors to his elegant consulting rooms.

Those clients who admired his polish and charm would have shuddered at the sight and smell of Fergus Trayle, in the condition in which Fergus had lived near Black Loch. Yet, if such admiring clients had themselves possessed an extra-sensory olfactory faculty, they would have been appalled by the moral stench of the fetid soul of the physically clean Cosmo Trayle. Where he was concerned, physical cleanliness was next to devilishness.

When Cosmo Trayle went into his private seance room that evening, Fergus was there waiting for him, now smelling considerably more wholesome than when in his own primitive habitat, since to take up quarters in Cosmo's house, Fergus had been obliged to go a long way towards satisfying his brother's fastidious requirements. But even so, anyone with that extra-sensory olfactory faculty would have vomited from the reek of sheer evil emanating from both brothers as they prepared the evening's seance.

71

Chapter Eight

Momentarily, the years have slipped away. It is war-time Britain.

Isa Strachan and Alec Vincent came out of the light, music and glamour of the Glasgow Empire, to stand hesitating on the entrance steps under the marquis. Reluctantly they relinquished the handclasp they had maintained through most of the variety show.

While they had been seated side by side in the theater, the handclasp had been invisible to other people. Now, however, they were on public view and King's Regulations forbade public hand-holding between members of His Majesty's Forces.

Had it been earlier or later in the year it would not have mattered so much, because then Sauchiehall Street would have been shrouded in the darkness of the wartime blackout. But in midsummer even wartime could not impose a blackout on an open street. So Isa had to remember that she was a subaltern in the Auxiliary Territorial Service, the women's Army. And she had to remember, too, that her companion was infantry officer Captain Alec Vincent.

Still, they looked a romantically handsome couple as they turned left for a stroll. They did not scramble for one of the few wartime taxis. They were in no particular hurry, both of them having passes entitling them to be out until midnight.

In Sauchiehall Street service uniforms almost equalled civilian outfits in number. Glasgow was the center of a concentration of the Forces. It was almost a nightly occurrence for messages to be flashed on movie screens recalling naval men in the audience to their ships for emergency action. The R.A.F. had its complement in the vicinity and the Army had almost taken over the city.

Isa was on the administrative staff at HQ Glasgow Area, and it was while on duty there that she had met Alec. He had been posted to Castle Douglas for Commando training, and had been obliged on several occasions to come to Glasgow Area HQ on administrative matters concerning Other Ranks in his Commando. It was almost like an act of Fate that Isa had been the officer delegated to deal with him.

On the surface it had been an unpromising setting for the beginning of a romance. The war atmosphere had been busy, grim purposeful. Wall charts with coded lists of units in the Area. Movement orders. Men going north to the troop transports, hospital ships and landing barges on Loch Fyne. All part of the gradual, painful build-up of men and materials for that eventual Second Front.

And, too, the bomb devastation among the tenements of Dumbarton as a constant reminder that Glasgow itself was in the firing line when the Luftwaffe could penetrate the anti-aircraft and fighter defenses.

Yet in a way this bustle and turmoil of war inspired feelings much like those in the days of knightly chivalry.

Often Isa felt like weeping at the sight of the boyish faces passing through Area HQ to their several destinies. No white armor and plumed helmets for them. Just the drab khaki of battledress. But what Saint George ever sallied forth with more enthusiasm to bar the marauding path of a fire-belching dragon?

Glasgow's canteens and clubs would live in the memories of many servicemen and women. The city had opened its heart to them.

As had Isa. Youthful servicemen had appealed to the maternal instinct in her—but it was Alec Vincent who had aroused her ardor.

Alec had come into her office with that unconscious slight swagger of the Commando man, born of the knowledge that he was one of the military elite. Picked, trained, ready and able to put the fear of hell into any Nazi who fancied his chance on level terms.

He had also worn a pistol at his belt, distinguishing him from administrative officers, who possessed sidearms but didn't wear them in the office.

The next thing which distinguished Alec Vincent was his immediate request for a date with her. Unlike her staff officer colleagues, he had no time in which to get to know her better, or as he put it, time to waste on formal applications in quadruplicate. His prospects were uncertain. He liked the look of Isa. So why wait?

He had got his date with her. And another—and another. Sometimes his plan for one had been frustrated when he couldn't get down from Castle Douglas—or could get down when she was not free. But the romance had flourished. For the very simple reason that they were in love.

It hardly needed saying that they intended to

marry. Their instinctive responses to each other had made that inevitable. Meanwhile they were extracting ecstatic happiness from their snatched meetings —like this one this evening.

They were still under the influence of the couple of hours' entertainment as they strolled up Sauchiehall Street past the scores of shops. The comedians' humor and the singers' melodies still echoed in their minds and the colorful stage lighting shed remembered brightness on the summer dusk.

When they came level with the yellow-tiled frontage of the Beresford Hotel they crossed the road and went inside for a drink—a toast to their mutual happiness. Both were aware that only together would they ever again know it.

With their drinks before them, they looked at each other across their table.

Isa, black-haired and pale-skinned, with long black lashes fringing her large dark eyes. Even her uniform could not make her less than arrestingly good-looking and feminine.

Alec, hair a golden auburn, skin slightly freckled, a twinkle in the blue eyes, a slanting grin curving the mouth.

He hailed a taxi to take her to her billet, and when they arrived, kept the taxi waiting as usual. It was now as near to being dark as it would ever be in this midsummer night.

For the first time she said to him, in her shadowed doorway, "You can send the taxi away—if you think it's worthwhile taking a chance on getting one . . . later."

After a perceptible pause he answered briefly, "It's worthwhile." And he ran down the steps and dismissed the cab.

A little later, in her bedroom, when he helped her remove her last obstructing garment, he said with amused appraisal of it:

"Mm—as glamorous as any of the chorus-girls' frillies tonight. But improper dress where an officer in uniform is concerned. Surely the regulation wear is khaki issue?"

She grimaced. "Those horrors! I couldn't face you in them."

Caressing her, he studied her face keenly.

"Then you were intending . . . tonight?"

"Well, we've both known we belong to each other. This only acknowledges it. Why should I deny you —or myself—the little we can be sure of? It wouldn't be honest for me to treat you as anything but my—"

He silenced her with a kiss that combined passion and affection.

Afterwards, lying beside her with his hand holding hers, he said thoughtfully: "You were right, of course. We've only underlined what was already written and understood." He lifted her left hand and said musingly, "I'll be putting a gold ring on this finger, though it can't mean any more than . . ."

As his hand clasped hers, her mind reeled dizzily —and the softly-lighted, austerely-furnished room lurched before her eyes. She was holding tight to his hand as her field of vision dimmed and shrank.

Shrank rapidly, to vanish into the darkness of oblivion . . .

. . . A dim pinpoint of red light expanded before Isa's gaze until a third of the room was vaguely visible to her.

The masculine hand was still in her grasp. A masculine hand. Somehow it felt different from Alec's.

Even her own hand felt different. Bonier. With a sensation of horror she realized that her whole body and face felt different.

She was sagging. Shoulders, breasts, the skin of her cheeks and throat. She felt tired, devitalized.

And the man who was holding her hand—he wasn't Alec. He was an older man, in civilian dress.

And past him—past and to one side—there was a tall black cabinet, in which another man was sitting, with his shaggy head flung back, his bearded chin tilted.

And then Isa Strachan was flooded with a realization of the bitter truth.

The man holding her hand was a civilian, and she too was a civilian. Now.

The man sitting facing her in the dim red glow, holding her hand, was Mr. Cosmo Trayle. This was his seance room.

And she was Miss Isa Strachan—aged forty-eight.

Until recent months it had been a quarter of a century since a man had held her hand. She knew that now. The illusion of the dead past, so briefly recalled, was now dispelled. Mr. Cosmo Trayle had just been holding her hand to establish a psychic *rapport*, so that he could convey her vibrations, amplified by his own psychic power, to the medium, his brother.

In those brief, far-off days of her happiness, a young man named Alec had held her hand for reasons of a more personal nature. Had he lived he would have placed a plain gold ring on her left hand and she wouldn't now have been known as Miss Strachan. She would have been Mrs. Alec Vincent.

But Alec hadn't lived. That evening the medium

had just recalled to vividly to her had been the very last she and Alec had spent together. Without its sweetness she would have had so much less to remember.

Next day Alec had been recalled to his unit for immediate movement with his Commando. Even she, who had taken the Official Secrets Act oath in common with the rest of Area HQ staff, was not able to learn his destination—until a daring raid somewhere on enemy-held territory announced it to the world.

By the time Isa had learned where Alec had gone, he was already dead, in his young manhood. In her memories he had never grown older. As her skin had sagged and begun to wrinkle and her hair to turn grey, he had remained unchanged. Of this she had just been reminded, with a bitter laceration of the heart, by that vivid vision of the time when they had both been young.

No other man had replaced Alec in her life. Through the decades her heart had contracted around her memories. When her parents had died she had sold their house in Dumfries and moved north to Glasgow, to give familiar substance to them.

Even when the Glasgow Empire had been demolished, other old haunts of hers and Alec's had remained, literally 'haunts'—tangible places which she could touch or walk upon again and so relive those brief days of war and love.

If only there had been more for her to recall in these bleak, lonely years of her middle-age!

With the passing of time even those precious few memories had dulled from sheer repetition. With no more to say and do than Alec had said and done during that distant courtship—a courtship too brief for her to have forgotten any detail of it—her life had kept playing itself out like an overly familiar strip of film.

Until Mr. Cosmo Trayle had made Alec a vivid, present reality, a voice with new things to say.

During the first consulation, when she had been desperate to learn through pyschometry what her remaining years held for her, Mr. Trayle had instantly sensed her chill emptiness. During the third consultation he had offered the only kind of help that could now comfort her. She was not to regard Alec as dead. The only real tragedy was that she had wasted so many years before learning this. Putting the bereaved in touch with their loved ones who had passed over was possible, through an ability shared by a few gifted mediums.

Some of these sensitives, Mr. Trayle mentioned casually, gave so much of their time to this noble work that earning an income from other sources was impossible. But usually those sorrowing people they helped expressed their gratitude in a practical way, so that their consolations might continue. . . .

At the thought of hearing Alec's voice again, that voice that had begun to fade, Miss Strachan had dismissed impatiently the importance of money. What happiness had her parents' legacy brought her? Of course a medium could not be expected to give his time gratis. Of course people with money ought to contribute enough to make up for those bereaved who could not afford to pay.

So, a couple of months ago, Mr. Cosmo Trayle had invited her to her first private seance. The officiating medium had been his own brother—a man who showed his spiritual nature by his indifference to the unkempt state of his hair and beard and the slovenliness of his clothes.

It was because of their family relationship, Mr. Cosmo had told Miss Strachan, that his brother had agreed to give her priority, despite his long waiting list. It was as a personal favor to Cosmo that Fergus was giving her a private sitting.

The first sitting had been a revelation.

In the dim red lighting of the darkened room, Cosmo had held her hand while his brother had gone into a trance. Because of the brothers' *rapport*, Miss Strachan's vibrations had passed to Fergus who had bridged the gulf between the living and those mistakenly regarded as dead.

Proof of Fergus's uncanny gift had been immediately forthcoming. His breathing had become heavier. Strange gurgles had come from his open mouth. The temperature of the room had dropped—sign of a presence from the Other Side.

The inarticulate gurgling had gradually resolved into intelligible words—faintly at first, then with more strength, so that she could tell the voice was masculine and young, with a definite Scots accent.

Mr. Cosmo Trayle had brought his mouth very close to her ear. He had whispered: "You recognise him?"

Miss Strachan had hesitated. So long ago . . . Who could tell whether even in her mental recollections the voice she 'heard' sounded exactly the same as the voice that had spoken to her so ardently a quarter of a century ago?

But when the voice issuing from the mouth of the entranced medium had appealed to her by name, doubt left her.

"Isa . . ." it said, still rather faintly but distinctly. "You're there, Isa . . . such a long time . . . Why have you never tried to get . . . in touch . . . before?"

Miss Strachan had felt guilty. Neglectful, thoughtless, faithless. The note of reproach in the voice had deepened her conviction that it was Alec's.

Tears had welled from her eyes. Suddenly she had shed the icy shroud of solitude, had come alive from her drab existence of so many years . . .

"Alec!" she had sobbed. "Alec . . ."

In subsequent seances she and Alec had renewed their old bond. Only at Mr. Trayle's was she now really alive. The time between seances was a dreary, meaningless interval of waiting.

Then had come hints from Alec that these waiting periods were quite unnecessary. He and she could be together completely and permanently.

New tones, as transmitted by the medium, began to convey his anguished sense of separation. They were communicating only by proxy. It was better than no communication at all, but it could not compare with their once vital intimacy.

Alec had revealed his frustration about a month ago, soon after she had confessed to Mr. Cosmo that she had bequeathed her entire fortune to him for the furtherance of his work.

By now she had come to be constantly tormented by the desire she shared with Alec. Her life alone was now desperate, for she had no prospects in this world but the bleak and the barren. In this world . . .

The gulf between herself and Alec could be crossed.

But not by Alec. Something he had said had made her realize that. He could not come to her. But she could go to him.

And what would be the point of prolonging the anguish of separation? Of seeing herself grow more and more decrepit, in contrast to Alec, who was forever young?

Tonight's seance, which had brought into sharp focus all her memories of those happy times in the same world with Alec, had finally decided her.

When she walked out of Mr. Cosmo Trayle's house her eyes were bright, exalted but remote. She was indifferent to the meaningless world now receding from her consciousness.

After the front door of the house had closed on her, Fergus Trayle came out of his cabinet and joined his brother in the consulting room, his bearded lips grinning.

"Well, Cosmo," he said bluntly, "it's now your turn to do something for me. I've just made certain you'll get that legacy with no more waiting. She'll even make it look like an accident, so you'll have no trouble in collecting the loot."

He was right.

Isa Strachan obliged her murderers by making her fatal fall in front of a moving Underground train at Bank Street Station look entirely accidental and unpremeditated.

She did it without fuss. It was only a few onlookers who screamed.

Chapter Nine

Donald Rathlaw prided himself on being a hard-headed, modern materialist.

He had been present when the unclean Hermit of Black Loch had uttered the curse on the Rathlaw family and predicted his own doom. And he had scoffed.

In University discussions with fellow undergraduates he had always been the skeptic when 'outlandish' theories had been debated. In his reaction against the traditions of his forebears and the mysticism of the Highlands, he was an intellectual iconoclast, with 'rational' explanations for any and all reports of the occult.

Even when his Uncle Malcolm had been struck blind and thereby fulfilled the Hermit's first prediction, Donald had refused to be impressed.

"All right," he said to his father, "so that stinker made a lucky guess. People are doing that on race-courses every day."

"But only because one horse in every race is bound to win," the Laird had replied. "That's a mathematical certainty, as you would say. But there was no mathematical certainty that a member of this family would be struck blind. Yet that fellow not only foresaw it happening, but predicted precisely which member of the family it would be. That's something more than just a lucky guess, lad!"

Intellectually Donald was stumped. But he was too stubborn to admit it.

Grinning, he had invited: "Go on, father—remind me of that water kelpie fairy-tale too. Tell me that makes him one hundred percent right about his omens. Only don't forget that the water kelpie's appearance is just hearsay—like the Irish and their leprechauns. It's never been scientifically proved that either kelpies or the little people exist."

Sir Alastair had frowned. "All right, discount the kelpie altogether if you like. But the lightning that blinded Malcolm was real enough. Real enough to make it commonsense for you to take great care—"

Again Donald had grinned.

"If that grimy scoundrel has the powers you credit him with, it won't do me much good, will it —to take care, I mean. You can't have it both ways, father. Either I'm doomed as he predicted, or what he said was a load of old rubbish. Either way, taking care would be a bit pointless—no matter how careful Malcolm might have been, he couldn't have guarded against that flash of lightning."

Uneasily Sir Alastair had retorted: "If he hadn't been using a steel-shafted club—"

"Aha! But even if he hadn't been using a steel-shafted club that day, he'd have been blinded some other way—if your fears about the Hermit's prophetic powers are justified. But I agree with you that the steel-shafted club was responsible—that's a scientific probability. Uncle wasn't the first golfer to pay dearly for carrying a steel-shafted club during a thunderstorm. But I still say the Hermit only made a lucky guess. And I'll tell you how and why."

"How?" Sir Alastair had challenged, puzzled.

"He made that prediction, father, simply because it was in the old Highland tradition. What did the curses of the old-time witches and warlocks always amount to? That somebody would be struck blind or die childless. And it stands to reason that if charlatans go on making two or three predictions often enough, eventually one of them is bound to coincide with fact. That's all there is to it—coincidence."

Feeling himself cornered, the Laird had to bring in mention of the second omen again.

"But *two* of the Hermit's predictions have come true. That water kelpie—"

Donald grinned derisively. "The Hermit knew the kind of people who were listening to him that night. And he knew how the news of his curse would spread. After his prediction of a water kelpie, it was a psychological certainty that sooner or later one of the superstitious locals would claim to have seen it. How many people have 'seen' the Loch Ness monster simply because there happens to be a legend that one exists?"

Sir Alastair had given up the argument and had consoled himself with the thought that perhaps it was best, after all, for the young man not to worry about the curse and the prophecies. But that had not prevented him from taking his worries to The Guardians.

When Steven Kane and Lionel Marks had arrived at the Castle, Donald had been too gentlemanly to pass any comment on their reason for coming. Though, in their absence, he had given his father an ironically chiding look.

Then he had gone to his room and played a beat record featuring performers so hard-headed and materialistic that they found their inspiration in the psychedelic fantasies produced by LSD.

When Steven Kane and Lionel Marks had left the Castle for an unmentioned destination, Donald went to Fiona's room. She was staying for a few days to settle details regarding their forthcoming wedding.

The invitation had been Sir Alastair's idea, based on the hope that her presence would keep his son safely at home. He should have known his son better.

Or perhaps he should have known Fergus Trayle better.

Whatever the subconscious prompting which urged Donald, he was in a mood to show how little he cared for the Hermit's curse and prophesies. And how better to show it than by going to Black Loch?

Fiona had been briefly introduced to Kane and Marks, but knew nothing of the reason for their presence, nor had Donald told her of the 'curse'. The servants had been forbidden to mention it to the girl and as her home was in Edinburgh, where Donald had first met her at the University, Fiona was still in ignorance of the threat hanging over him.

Certainly Donald's face, when she opened her door in response to his tap, showed no signs of worry.

"Hello, darling," he greeted her. "Feel like a run in the fresh air?"

She smiled. She was not surprised that he wanted to take her off somewhere so that they could be alone for a while.

"Of course, Donald. How should I dress?"

He tweaked her nose. "Women! Just as you are of course. We're going across the estate in a Land Rover, not up The Mall in a limousine."

"Then I'll put on a headscarf and powder my nose—"

Lounging against the doorpost, he gave an exhibition of manly patience while she made those essential feminine preparations. Then he took her down to the courtyard and installed her in one of the front seats of the Land Rover.

To the challenge of Black Loch's reputation he added the conscious excuse that going there would take them away from the knowing eyes of his father's employees and tenants. If a fellow couldn't have a bit of privacy with the girl he was going to marry . . .

"You'll make a good wife," he told her smilingly, as they sped along the rutted road. "Like the pioneer women you see in Westerns—prepared to follow their man into the wilderness."

Seated beside him, she glanced up into his smooth, handsome face as though she sensed some special serious significance in his jocular remark. Then she snuggled closer to him.

"Till death us do part," she assured him, with fond solemnity.

And then, for some reason, she shivered.

By the time they had left the Rathlaw estate behind and were traversing the slope of the Black Glen, Donald had recovered his self-assurance. All the superstitions associated with remote places were simply the results of silence, grim terrain and somber 'atmosphere.' The few people in these primitive places had nothing to distract their minds from the oppressive effect of bleak and hushed surroundings.

On impressionable minds and fertile imaginations such an environment could work wonders of fantasy. People saw a monster in remote Loch Ness, but nobody ever saw one in the River Thames.

Donald deliberately closed his mind to the logical thought that aquatic monsters and evil men could have reason to avoid thickly populated areas. So the corollary thought did not occur to him—that men who found in remote places the necessary privacy for their evil deeds could in time, by those deeds, give such places a sinister reputation. The remoteness would thus be only an indirect cause of the reputation.

To Donald's stubborn streak, the Hermit's curse was simply a challenge, with no risk.

Here he was on what had been the Hermit's own territory, approaching the place where the alleged water-kelpie had been seen. And what was there to worry about? Nature was neutral. Steep and craggy geological formations and the fact that water collected in a valley had no metaphysical significance. If few people came here, that was merely because there were no special aesthetic attractions to compensate for the discomfort and difficulty of traveling from the towns and cities. Ordinary cars would simply get stranded with broken springs.

But it was an ideal place for a fellow with a Land Rover to come when he could bring the desired aesthetic attractions with him in the shape of his girl. Young men in city parks didn't realize what they were missing, dating their girls among the passing throng and the metallic moan of portable radios.

There was nothing here in Black Glen to distract him from Fiona. She had the blue eyes and fresh complexion that so often accompanied red hair. She was wearing a thin shift dress which she had not bothered to change because the weather was mild.

Her shoes too were of city style, though with the stubby heels fashion had decreed for wear with a short dress, so that they were quite suitable for a stroll beside the Loch. Only her outfit, though suitable for these conditions, was much more appealing than a country outfit of tweed suit and brogues would have been. So Donald was relaxed and content.

As he drove across the Glen slope, she commented: "Not the gayest of places, darling."

He grinned. "We've brought the gaiety with us. With only three days to go, I'm loaded with it!"

He turned down the hill and drove slowly towards the Loch shore, surrounded for most of its extent by pine woods.

Had the weather remained overcast, he would have been plunging into a valley of gloom, for the encircling hills shut out much of the sky. But just as he turned down the hillside the evening sun broke through the veil of cloud, to send mellow light flooding down onto the dimness of the Loch, making its smooth surface glisten.

Smiling, Fiona said. "Is that your gaiety—or an omen?"

He flashed her a startled glance. But that glance told him she had spoken quite innocently. Had she known of the two sinister omens she would not have used the word in a jocular way.

For a couple of seconds, however, Donald felt uneasy. Then he admitted to himself that he felt better for the sudden brightness. But it only confirmed, he thought, that people were frightened by shadows and made morbidly imaginative by 'atmosphere.' When sunlight did get through the hilltop mist, even Fiona spoke of an omen—a good one.

Donald began to whistle a current pop tune. When the Land Rover reached the level shore of the Loch he braked, switched off the engine, then ran around the front of the vehicle to catch Fiona around the waist as she jumped down. She had been looking up at the pine woods, covering the lower slopes of the Glen in nearly every direction, but he had eyes only for her. His whistle became one of joyous admiration. "Mine—all mine," he grinned, slowly allowing her feet to touch ground. He crushed her to him until she was breathless.

"Next week, my lad," she smiled, struggling free.

He turned, reached into the back of the Land Rover and brought out a tartan car-rug.

Fiona eyed him askance as he carefully spread it out over a patch of moss and pine needles. "I thought we'd be having some healthy exercise after that long ride," she said pointedly.

"We're going to," he said, reaching up from where he was kneeling to grasp one of her hands.

"I meant a stroll around the Loch—" she began. But he pulled her down beside him and took her in his arms, smothering her upturned face with kisses.

At the beginning of their very short engagement, Fiona had told him that she never gave birthday presents beforehand and that she labeled all Yuletide gifts 'Not to be opened before Christmas.' Birthdays and Christmas, she stated, would otherwise seem flat. She had intimated that she intended to follow that policy during their engagement and make sure that the honeymoon would not be an anti-climax.

As her own nature was warm, it was probable that she would not have followed the policy had there been much longer than three days to wait. But wait now she would. When Donald looked as though he had reached a certain boiling-point she wriggled free, got to her feet and walked away, leaving him simmering.

For over a minute he lay there disgruntled, propped on an elbow, watching her strolling along beside the Loch. Her headscarf had slipped off and lay on the rug, and her hair, now ruffled, glowed brightly in the sunlight. She was such an attractive picture that he lazily and gradually forgot his disappointment.

It was only when the sunlight was abruptly blotted out by a thickening cloud that he aroused himself and got to his feet.

The surrounding pinewoods suddenly looked black, as did the surface of the Loch. Fiona's hair was no longer so vivid—and she herself seemed to be much further away.

A chill swept across the valley.

Donald called after the receding girl: "Hey, Fiona! Wait for me—"

She did not stop. Neither did she look back. Instead her pace quickened.

As Donald was about to run after her, she veered to her right and continued walking—directly towards the edge of the Loch.

He hesitated. His surprise changed to sheer astonishment and alarm as she walked right into the shallow water lapping the shore—walked into it with her shoes on.

His hesitation was brief. But by then the water was up to her calves and she was still walking. He took off in a sprint to overtake her. Now that she had changed direction he could see her face in profile. She was staring straight ahead of her, walking steadily out into deeper water, and by the time he reached the shore she was up to her thighs—an erect, solitary figure walking deliberately to a suicide's death, three days before her wedding.

Chapter Ten

Donald, horror-stricken, splashed through the shallow in-shore waves. Fiona was well down the shelving's outer depth and stolidly ploughing on. When he grabbed her the water was above her shoulders, and she was not swimming, or even trying to.

Her eyes were blank. He jumped ahead of her to swing her around. It was if she were sleep-walking.

An unearthly pallor on her cheeks and the frozen stillness of her lips brought Donald to the edge of panic.

"Fiona!" he got out hoarsely.

In the unnatural twilight her face was a ghastly mask which seemed to be floating bodilessly on Loch's ebony surface.

She looked at Donald—and through him.

For a couple of seconds he stood with water lapping his chest, staring into her face and gripping her hard by the shoulders. Not the water swirling around him nor the girl sent the sudden shiver up his spine, but something eerier that he could not explain. Suddenly he reached down under her knees and swung her up into his arms.

The shift dress was clinging wetly to her body as he strode ashore and trotted rapidly towards the Land Rover. As he reached it, Fiona seemed to recover, perhaps from being carried in his arms. The blank look faded. She stared up at his face in wonder, her normal intelligence restored.

"Donald! What's up? Why are you carrying me—?"

"Skip the questions for now, darling," he said crisply. "You've got to get into dry things, quickly. And you're going to have a medical check-up. I'm going to make certain that you do."

He stood her down near the tartan car-rug. "Get those wet things off!" he ordered.

She clasped her bare arms around herself, shivering. He looked at her, his brows drawn together in a frown.

"Do you want to get penumonia?" he demanded. "Get those things off and give them to me. Then wrap the rug round you and dry yourself thoroughly. Hurry!"

Under his commanding eye Fiona took off her wet dress and undergarments, then her shoes. Donald started the engine, and as it heated, dried the clothes somewhat on the Land Rover's hood. He went back then to Fiona, who was now wrapped in the car-rug with only her head and ankles showing and, before she could speak, swung her up into his arms and deposited her on the car's front seat. He climbed in beside her.

"Tuck your feet up inside the rug," he said. "If

you can't manage it, I'll try to rub some warmth into them."

She found that, seated, she could get the rug down around her feet. But her gaze was on his face, asking him questions, and she put the questions into words.

"What was that you said about my seeing a doctor? I'll be all right now that I'm dry. Everybody gets wet after a swim."

Quietly Donald said: "You haven't been swimming. You were sleep-walking."

"Sleep-walking!" she repeated, and her voice held a note of incredulity.

"That's right. You walked right into the Loch with your eyes open. Do you make a habit of sleep-walking, or were you just trying to get out of marrying me—the hard way?" He spoke lightly, but watched her closely.

Half-turned towards him she shook her head in bewilderment.

"But I don't understand! I've never sleep-walked in my life!"

"Then you must have gone into some kind of trance," he said. "Don't you remember walking into the Loch?"

She shook her head again. "No. All I remember is that I was strolling along by the water, waiting for you to come after me. Just before the sun went in I remember feeling . . . depressed. And cold. The next thing is that you were carrying me. I tell you, Donald—I've never walked in my sleep before. Ever!"

"You're quite sure of that?" he persisted. "Not even when you were a child? Some girls have what they call pre-wedding nerves, you know—and if you'd ever sleep-walked as a child, any kind of tension could revive it."

"No," she said again, and her voice was resolute. "Besides, people who sleep-walk do it when they're asleep—after they've gone to bed, I mean. Not in broad daylight! I was walking along by the water, I tell you—and that's all I remember. Do you think—" She looked at him a little apprehensively now—"do you think I could have had a mental . . . black-out, Donald?"

"It's possible," he said seriously. "But the fact that you did so while you were actually walking isn't the only queer thing about it. If you'd carried on walking in the same direction, you wouldn't have put such a scare into me! But you turned and walked right into the Loch. When I reached you the water was nearly up to your chin—if I'd been further away, or slower . . ."

She met his anxious gaze and for the first time since he had known her, Donald saw she was frightened. He forced a rather shaky smile.

"Maybe it's just that you aren't so keen on getting married as you think you are," he said jokingly. "Your subconscious is urging you to walk out on me. But I'd rather see you marry some other man than try to commit suicide—"

"Donald!" The fear lurking in her eyes was banished by a sudden glisten of unshed tears. "You know that isn't true! I'm looking forward to our wedding-day just as much as you are!" She forced a smile. "Perhaps what just happened was a throw-back to the 'vapors' grandma used to get when she thought of her honeymoon!"

"I still think you ought to see a doctor," he said doggedly.

"No, darling. Don't look so worried. I've no suicidal intentions at all, I assure you. You said yourself that I appeared to be sleep-walking when I walked into the Loch, which seems proof enough that I didn't know what I was doing. It was purely by accident I turned—don't people always walk in a circle when they can't see?"

"What d'you mean—when they can't see? Couldn't *you* see, Fiona? If you couldn't, that proves you were asleep—and we should find out why—"

She reached out and put her hand upon his knee. "Lets make a bargain, darling. If anything like this ever happens again, then I'll see a doctor right away. I promise. But if it's never going to happen again—and I can't see any reason why it should—then there's no sense in upsetting everyone, is there?" She added, slyly: "Besides, I won't be able to cheat—because in three days' time you'll be able to keep a personal eye on me, day and night."

He chuckled. "I suppose that's fair enough."

"Of course it is!" She spoke briskly now. "The only tonic I need is a honeymoon." She glanced out at the gloom-shrouded valley. "This place could give anybody a fit of the blues, couldn't it?"

He nodded, smiling. "There's a lot in what you say, sweetheart. The atmosphere's not exactly conducive to a cheerful frame of mind. Tomorrow I'll run you into Aberdeen for a day of noisy, uncomplicated fun—Scotland's leading holiday resort should buck you up."

She peered out through the windscreen. "My clothes are beginning to steam, Donald. I'd better get into them—"

"If they're steaming they can't be dry," he objected. "Worse thing you could do. You'll be warmer if I take you back to the Castle in that rug—"

"And have the servants jumping to conclusions about how I lost my clothes?"

"We'll tell them the truth, naturally—"

She gave what could only be described as a ladylike snort. "If you tell them I walked into the Loch fully dressed they'll start tapping their heads—and I couldn't blame them. You don't want people to think you've picked yourself someone who's *non compos mentis*, do you?"

"Darling! We can simply say that you tripped and fell into the shallow edge of the Loch—"

"Oh, yes! And tell them also why you brought me to this God-forsaken place—that should make them smirk!"

He nodded, conceding the point. "Okay, then," he said reluctantly. "We'll just have to wait until your clothes are dry—considering there's so little of them, that shouldn't take long."

It didn't. After a third test Donald announced they were dry enough for her to put on. He brought them to her.

"Thanks," she said. "For bundling them up like that, I mean. A few dozen wrinkles improves any dress. I wouldn't be surprised if the dress has shrunk too much for me to get it on, anyway."

"There's only one way to find out. Hop into the back and try it."

"Of course—it's so easy to 'hop into the back,' wrapped up like an Eskimo—"

Patiently he said: "You'll have to take the rug off then, won't you. Go on. I'll keep an eye on you."

"That," she said, "I am prepared to believe."

And she dropped the rug and clambered palely into the back of the Land Rover, where in the shelter of its hood she dressed under his dutifully watchful eye.

"So that's how the mini-dress was invented," he commented. The hem of the shrunken dress reached only to her stocking tops. "Ah well, if the servants are about when we get back, you'd better make a quick dash for your room. Seeing you like this isn't one of their privileges—"

As soon as she had returned to her seat beside him, Donald started the vehicle and drove up out of the valley.

It was comforting for him to realize that the Loch's oppressive effect was in one's mind only. Because had he not been so hard-headed, he admitted to himself, this climb back up the side of the Glen would have been like emerging from some pit of a nether world, with a lake of mephitic black pitch ringed by stark sentinels.

Then, as the Land Rover sped back across the hillside to open country and the Rathlaw estate, Donald told himself that his sigh of relief signified only that the worst part of the driving was now over.

He was only too pleased to accept Fiona's suggestion that her strange aberration had been due to some form of mental 'black-out'—a nervous reaction perhaps, not to be repeated.

That it had been anything else he dared not believe.

Next morning Donald and Fiona made an early start and reached Aberdeen in time to park the car and take a stroll along the esplanade of the two-mile pleasure beach before lunch.

The sand was crowded with holiday-makers, and

Fiona particularly enjoyed the sight of the children frolicking in their own beach Playpen.

"I wonder how many *we'll* have," she mused, as she and Donald paused to watch the fun.

"How many what?"

"Children, of course, you ninny!"

Donald hesitated. Then, defiantly, he said: "Oh—at least six."

She looked at him curiously. "You said that in a challenging sort of way, darling. Did you think I wouldn't want any?"

"No, of course not. What an idea!" Quickly he changed the subject. "Here, let's go and find one of the ten-pin bowls, shall we?"

"Just as you like. I bet all the lanes are booked up, though . . ."

They found that all thirty lanes in the George Street bowling center had indeed been reserved and were in use. So after watching for a while they had drinks in the lounge bar, where, a few minutes later Fiona leaned towards Donald and said in an undertone:

"Do you ever get the feeling you're being watched?"

He grinned at her. "Occasionally. But it must be a regular experience for you." In her lime-green shirt and dark green tapered slacks, she was definitely eye-catching.

"I don't mean by the ordinary devoted bird-watchers, darling. One gets to be able to spot them —and enjoys seeing them turn sheepish when they realise they've been spotted. No—this feeling I've had a couple of times in the last half-hour—it's more . . . more intimidating than that."

He saw that she was quite serious. Casually he

glanced around the crowded lounge, but saw no one paying her any particular attention. Again he tried to make a joke of it.

"You won't have committed bigamy, Fiona, when we get hitched? You haven't a husband tucked away somewhere, have you? If so, it's quite possible that the Law's on your tail, now that our wedding date has been publicly announced."

She smiled to match his teasing.

"I'll answer that question on our wedding night," she said lightly. "Let's get some fresh air, shall we?"

"Certainly." He finished his drink. They returned to the sea front and watched a Beach Leader showing some youngsters how to build a sand castle.

Fiona said pensively: "I'd hate it, Donald, if we didn't have any children."

He raised his eyebrows in protest. "Are you casting doubts on my virility, my girl? Have no fear. My father is counting on us to present him with a grandson next spring. Would I let him down—or you?" Somehow, even to Donald himself, his jocularity seemed forced. He felt uneasy.

Suddenly Fiona shivered. He looked at her anxiously. "Not starting a chill are you, in this sunshine?"

"I . . . no. I had that feeling again, of being watched. And by somebody who doesn't feel very friendly towards me . . ."

She glanced around, then turned back to him with a shrug. "Just my morbid fancy," she muttered. "Probably from being among so many people after that deserted place we visited yesterday."

Donald grimaced and took her arm, continuing their stroll along the esplanade. "I brought you here to make you forget Black Loch," he said sternly. "What we need is some strenuous activity, not all this mind-searching. What shall it be? You name it, we'll do it."

"Swimming," she suggested.

"No swimming," he said firmly.

"Why ever not?"

"And no arguments."

"Oh, stuff!" she replied impatiently. Then she staggered. From among the many people on the esplanade, a small boy had dashed impetuously and collided with her. But while Fiona only staggered, the boy fell sprawling to his hands and knees.

They looked down at him in concern. As he tried to scramble up they could see that his bare knees were grazed and beginning to bleed slightly. But, curiously, he did not cry. Donald bent down and helped the boy to his feet. He appeared to be about ten years old. His tow-like hair hung in an untrimmed fringe nearly down to his large round eyes, giving his face an elfish expression.

Fiona asked: "Are you hurt much, laddie?"

He mutely shook his head.

"Sure?" Donald insisted.

Ignoring him, the boy continued to gaze up at Fiona. He opened his mouth and pointed into it with a finger, making a faint hissing sound.

"Oh, Donald!" Fiona exclaimed, her eyes widening with pity. "The poor boy is—" She broke off, afraid of embarrassing the youngster, then stooped down. "Let me see to those knees, eh?" she suggested hurriedly.

With her handkerchief she brushed off the layer of dust on the grazed knees, leaving him to wipe off

101

the blood. Then, smiling, she said: "They must be sore. I know—let me buy you an ice-cream?"

The boy hesitated, then shook his head, but there was an almost pleading expression on his face.

"What, then?" she asked. "Candyfloss?"

Again he shook his head. Then he pointed down to the beach, towards a group of ponies carrying vociferous young riders along the sand.

"Oh, you'd like a pony ride?" with an understanding smile, Fiona glanced about the esplanade. "Well, I don't know where your folks are—not lost, are you?"

The boy's negative headshake was vigorous.

"Then of course you shall have a pony ride!" Fiona assured him. "Come along, Donald—"

She took hold of one of the boy's small hands and led the way. Donald smiled. If a maternal instinct promised anything, his father should be having his hoped-for grandson—and a few more to follow.

They reached the steps leading down to the beach and trudged along the crowded sands towards the start of the pony rides, where a few animals were tethered feeding on hay. The mute boy patted their sleek necks with self-assurance. They stopped feeding to look at him and whinny softly.

Donald glanced at Fiona in amused surprise. "What about that! They took to him right away."

"No wonder he wanted a ride," Fiona smiled. "He knows ponies."

The lad picked up a length of straw from near the main bale of hay, and while waiting, stuck one end in his mouth and chewed it.

A moment later four ponies returned with their riders and the two teenage lads in charge.

102

Other prospective customers joined the group. Fiona paid for her temporary protege's ride and Donald offered to help him mount.

The boy shook his head and easily got on his chosen pony unaided. When three other customers were in the saddle to complete the quartet, the boys in charge turned the ponies to begin the new ride.

Just as they were starting off the dumb boy, with a strange smile, leaned towards Fiona and playfully flung the straw into her face. She laughed good-naturedly. The ponies trotted off along the sand.

When they came back a few minutes later only three of the four ponies still had riders. The dumb lad's pony now had an empty saddle.

One of the youths in charge said to Fiona: "Your boy? Oh, he reined in and hopped off at the end of the outward run. Disappeared among the crowd."

"Saddle-sore already?" Donald grinned. "He isn't our boy. Probably he spotted his folks." He took Fiona's arm and they went back to the esplanade.

Fiona had not yet realized that the dumb lad still had her handkerchief.

And neither she nor Donald knew that, in the occult lore of the Highlands, to fling a wisp of straw into an enemy's face was the way to drive him—or her—insane.

Chapter Eleven

Very thoughtfully Lionel Marks watched Donald Rathlaw and Fiona returning to the esplanade. He took great care that they should not see him.

He had witnessed the collision between Fiona and young Jamie Erskine—for the simple reason that he had been following Jamie and his mother, Aggie. He had followed them all the way from Black Loch.

Having pin-pointed Cosmo Trayle's house, he and Steven Kane had kept a close watch on it. And when early that morning Cosmo had got into his car and driven north, Marks, on his trail, had to his astonishment found him driving directly to the Black Glen and to the Erskine farmhouse. When Cosmo entered it, Marks had hidden his own car among trees some distance away and watched through field-glasses. Even as he waited he was aware of an uncomfortable feeling along his spine and had an inclination to glance uneasily over his shoulder, as though expecting at any moment some mysterious manifestation.

When Cosmo finally left the farmhouse. he had Aggie Erskine and Jamie with him, leaving Marks considerably puzzled as to why the weak-minded croft woman and her young son had been collected —in person, by the suave cosmopolite.

He had taken it for granted that Cosmo would return to Glasgow, but on leaving Black Glen, Trayle headed directly south-east towards Aberdeen. Intrigued, Marks followed cautiously. Why on earth, he wondered, had Cosmo Trayle made a long journey north and a shorter one south-east in connection with the Erskines? What could they do that Cosmo himself could not have done?

At the sea front, Cosmo slowly toured the street, obviously searching for somebody. By that time it was afternoon and Marks was feeling not only tired but hungry and untidy. He had not dared stop on the way for fear of losing his quarry.

Suddenly Cosmo Trayle had stopped his car and deposited Aggie and Jamie on the esplanade. They presented an incongruous pair. They had apparently washed before leaving the farmhouse, but were as shabbily dressed as before, in startling contrast to Cosmo's elegante. Marks could well understand why Trayle had remained in the car after disgorging his passengers.

The collision between young Jamie and Fiona came as a surprise to Marks, for he had not known the girl was in Aberdeen. But had Cosmo known—and how?

The question made Marks smile wryly. How had Steven Kane known that Fergus Trayle was in Glasgow? As occultists, the two Trayle brothers would have resources as uncommon as Kane's.

Either Cosmo or Fergus had divined Donald's intention to visit Aberdeen—had foreseen the couple's stroll near the sea front. So sure of it had Cosmo been that his long drive for the Erskines was guaranteed to produce results. The fact that Cosmo had begun the trip even before Donald Rathlaw and the girl had left the Castle proved the accuracy of his extraordinary fore-knowledge.

So Lionel Marks then had a grim sense of foreboding. For if Cosmo Trayle knew in advance what Donald and Fiona had intended doing that day, Donald's hopes of immunity from the Hermit's plans seemed doomed.

For the first time, perhaps, Marks realized the full extent of the Trayle brothers' powers and the evil forces against which he and Steven Kane were preparing to do battle. And he had a very real fear for young Donald Rathlaw.

When Cosmo Trayle turned the two Erskines out of his car like a huntsman unleashing a couple of hounds, Marks had been in something of a dilemma. Whom to follow—Trayle himself, or the grotesque mother and her son?

But the dilemma had been only momentary because on reaching the esplanade, Aggie Erskine had hung back—and her son had darted into the moving throng alone.

His collision with Fiona Ross had come almost immediately, from which Marks judged that Trayle had seen her and Donald seconds before letting the Erskines out. And since the active job had been delegated to Jamie, it was Jamie on whom Marks now concentrated.

Marks slipped out of the MG and mingled with the strollers. He was aware that Cosmo Trayle immediately drove away and that Aggie lost herself somewhere in the crowd. But Marks's beady eyes were fixed on Jamie, Fiona and Donald, and he had no further time to spare for Cosmo or the Erskine woman.

Several holiday-makers were studying the sea and the beach through telescopes and binoculars and there was nothing conspicuous in Marks's use of his own field glasses to watch Donald and Fiona taking young Jamie down to the beach.

Marks saw in close-up the incident of the wisp of straw flung into Fiona's face, and young Jamie's strange expression during the unexpected action. It was the same almost malicious joy which Jamie had bestowed upon him following the incident of the supposed kelpie, and Marks felt the same swift unease.

He was much less erudite concerning Highland witchcraft than Steven Kane was. But he was too experienced to dismiss the straw-flinging as of no significance.

But Marks was left guessing, just as Donald and Fiona were, when Jamie did not return with the other pony riders. Moreover, he was irritated that the boy had given him the slip. His only consolation was that so far neither Donald nor Fiona had come to any harm.

It seemed absurd to suppose that any harm could result from their brief encounter with a ten-year-old boy. But—remembering only too clearly his own experience of Jamie's uncanny powers in the ramshackle Erskine farmhouse—Marks knew that it was no ordinary boyish mentality which looked out of those large round eyes.

He wondered what to do—whether to hunt for Cosmo Trayle and the Erskines, or follow Donald and Fiona.

In the end he left the decision to Steven Kane.

Kane had stayed behind in Glasgow to keep an eye

on Cosmo Trayle's house, for by this time both he and Marks were aware that Fergus was there. With binoculars they had glimpsed him for a brief moment in the rear garden, in company with his brother. Even at that distance the likeness between them was striking, and Kane knew that he was on the right track.

It had been arranged that Kane would be in a public phone-booth close to Cosmo's house at certain times of the day. Marks had rung him once, but missed him. This time, after following Donald and Fiona to a restaurant, he made a trunk call to Glasgow and got through.

Marks gave Kane a rapid resume of events.

"The question is, what do I do now? Keep with young Donald and the girl—or try to pick up Cosmo's trail again. There's a possibility, of course, that I may be able to do both. If Trayle is still keeping tabs on them, he's bound to show himself again—"

"I think it's a very strong possibility," said Kane. "It's hardly likely he brought the Erskines all the way to Aberdeen simply so that Jamie could fling a straw into Fiona's face! You saw nothing else significant?"

Marks hesitated. "I did notice that after Fiona had dabbed at young Jamie's knees with her handkerchief, the boy took it from her and wiped them himself."

Kane's voice was edged with sudden sharpness. "What did he do with the handkerchief afterwards? Did he return it?"

"No. He stuffed it into his pocket in an absent-minded sort of way—"

"In an absent-minded sort of way, perhaps, but

not absent-mindedly," said Kane positively. "The action was deliberate—and even more important than what he did with the straw. Remember what *I* managed to do with the help of a matchbox which had been handled by the Hermit?"

Marks felt bound to protest. "But, hang it all, the Trayles didn't need that handkerchief to locate Fiona and Donald. Even without it they knew they would be going to Aberdeen!"

"So they want the handkerchief for some other purpose—and a more deadly one at that. As a psychometrist, friend Cosmo will be able to learn much from that handkerchief about Fiona and people important to her. And God knows what use Fergus may be able to make of an article which has had her personal contact." He was silent for a moment, thinking deeply, then he said with a slow deliberation in his voice: "Lionel—this makes it absolutely imperative that you should keep close to Donald and the girl."

Once more Lionel Marks was acutely conscious of the evil powers of the men they were fighting. He said quickly: "You can depend on me, Steven—"

"Don't let them know you're following them," said Kane. "And if you see Cosmo in their vicinity, find some way of telephoning me. You can reach me at any time during the next two hours at our Glasgow hotel—"

"By my life, do you mean to say you've abandoned the watch on the Trayles' house?" asked Marks, in consternation.

Kane gave a short laugh. "On the contrary, I've now organized an unbroken, round-the-clock surveillance. Just after you left this morning I phoned London and asked Anne to fly up to Renfrew Airport, five miles from here. She'll be taking over at the Trayles' house, in about fifteen minutes from now, while I snatch a rest—"

"What about tonight?" asked Marks.

"I'll be keeping watch. If you phone the hotel during the night, Anne will cope."

"I see . . ."

Kane sensed the dubious note. He said: "Lionel, there's an aura of almost palpable evil around Trayle's house. And it didn't noticeably diminish when Cosmo left this morning. My belief is that this aura emanates almost entirely from Fergus. Evil as Cosmo undoubtedly is, I think his brother can teach him something about devilry. We must keep in mind the fact that it was Fergus who cursed the Rathlaws, who hates the Laird and young Donald. Whatever agents he may use, he is the arch-enemy—and we mustn't forget that, even for a moment."

Marks's tone was unusually subdued. "If Fergus actually begot that boy—and his powers are even more impressive than his offspring's—then, by the Lord Harry, I'm only too glad *you're* handling things at his end!"

Marks got off the phone in time to see Donald and Fiona finish their meal. When they left the restaurant, he sensed that they were about to drive back to Rathlaw, a belief strengthened when, following, he saw them stop at a gas station and fill the Land Rover tank.

Noting the direction they took, Marks made a quick job of filling his own tank, and went off in pursuit.

As Marks was fond of relating, his career had consisted largely of lurking, tailing and key-holing. He expertly overhauled the young couple and within a few miles had confirmation of his guess that they were on their way home.

That wasn't his only guess. His conversation with Kane had made it clear to him that if Fergus Trayle intended to 'get at' Donald for the purpose of ensuring that his fatal prediction came true, he intended to do so through Fiona. Either she was to be the means of bringing about Donald's death—or, not content with the prospect of that young man's premature demise—Fergus Trayle planned to dispose of Fiona also.

Before his own death, Donald was intended to see Fiona suffer or die.

The flick in the face with a wisp of straw had been, Kane declared, with the intent of driving the recipient insane. But it seemed ridiculous to suppose that such an action, of itself, could have this effect. Probably it had merely been symbolic—and would be backed up by the concentrated malignancy of Fergus's distorted mind.

Who knew what dark powers could accrue to such a mind, brooding in solitude on its grievances? Who even knew what additional powers Fergus had developed during the year since he had uttered that curse?

To make the curse come true by murdering Donald would be simple. But that was not the way the Hermit of Black Loch would work. Even Sir Alastair had realized that, or he would not have sought the aid of the Guardians.

Donald was intended to die in fear—in superstitious terror. That had been the purpose of the two omens. To let him know that his doom was approaching; to cause him to spend his last weeks or months in suspense and dread.

To all appearances the omens had failed to have that effect. Superficially, Donald was a man as happy as a young man should be a few days before his wedding, and in the company of the girl who was to be his bride.

But the Trayles had not rested content with the omens. Today's events had shown that they were on the offensive—in their own devious, esoteric ways.

Lionel Marks's job, he reminded himself, was to make sure that Donald and the girl got safely back to Rathlaw Castle. Once there, he and Kane could deal with further developments between them.

When Aberdeen had been left well behind and the traffic thinned on the north-west road into the Highlands, Marks's eyes flickered continually on the lookout for Cosmo Trayle's car—with or without the Erskines. But he saw nothing of it.

By the time darkness had fallen Marks and the car he was following had left the A944 major road and were speeding north-west on a narrow third-class road through the wilds. It was obviously going to be a late hour when Donald and Fiona rolled up to the gates of Rathlaw Castle.

Following their car was much easier now that its tail-lights were switched on, and were the only ones visible. Marks relaxed a little, succumbing to the tiredness which was beginning to stretch his nerves almost to breaking-point. He would be glad when this final stage of the journey was over and he could rest . . .

Nothing showed in his rear-view mirror but a blank black vista of empty road behind him. His own

MG and Donald's car were the only two spearing their headlights into the darkness.

They were six miles from the boundary of the Rathlaw estate when it happened.

Since the two cars had the road to themselves, Marks had dropped back in order not to seem to be hugging Donald's car too obviously.

It was into this respectable gap, at the far reach of his headlights, that the woman staggered.

She stumbled drunkenly out of the darkness at the right of the road and fell sprawling face-down across the center. There was no room at either side of the road for Marks to pass her, even if he had tried to do so.

After so many miles of steady, uninterrupted cruising, the sudden and unexpected occurrence made Marks's heart lurch violently. But he managed to bring the MG to a stop without veering. Leaving the motor ticking over he opened the nearside door and climbed out.

His senses fatigued, Marks's thoughts were far removed from any possible hint of danger as he walked towards the prone woman. He felt angry rather than apprehensive—some crofter's wife, he supposed, drunk on liquor illicitly distilled in some secret hiding-place among the hills. It could happen.

He bent his head to look at the woman more closely. But before he could speak she suddenly squirmed around and sat up.

She was no woman. It was grotesque, but she was no woman. The merest glance showed Marks that. It was a man's face that was gazing up at him.

As he looked into that face Marks's heart seemed to thump a rapid tattoo against his ribs. For, glinting in the beams of the MG's headlamps, were the weirdly unmatched eyes of Cosmo Trayle.

For a moment Marks thought he was in the grip of some fantastic nightmare. Donald's car had vanished into the darkness ahead, but here—sitting in the center of the road and glaring up at him—was Cosmo Trayle, clad grotesquely in a woman's blouse and skirt, his trouser-legs pulled farcically up above his knees, his hair ruffled to give a momentary illusion of a woman's.

Magnetically his odd eyes held Marks in their focus. Then, like a night creature scurrying out of the hedgerow, a small figure scampered into the area of illumination.

It was the dumb boy, Jamie Erskine.

To complete the trio, with the crowning touch of farce, a woman came out on to the lighted road, giggling coyly—the coyness presumably being due to the fact that she was dressed only in a grimy camisole.

And that, presumably, explained where Cosmo Trayle had obtained his blouse and skirt.

Marks tensed, for once hardly knowing what to do. He had been taken completely off his guard. The scene was too fantastic—Cosmo Trayle sitting on the ground in blouse and skirt, like some female impersonator in a crude amateur knock-about, but gazing up at him malevolently, with a stare which clove Marks's tongue dryly to the roof of his mouth.

Jamie, grinning and staring at Marks saucer-eyed, making eerie hisses of excitement.

And the tall, giggling, half-dressed woman advancing on Marks as if with amorous designs on him.

But the action she took when within reach of him was the reverse of amorous. It came as a complete surprise because it had not occurred to Marks that a woman would attack him with her bare hands—or even attack him at all.

And when her hands closed around his throat he reacted too late.

Their strength was a frightening revelation; her grip was like that of a professional strong man. And as Marks beat at her wrists to dislodge them he could still see the unmatched eyes of the crazily-dressed man sitting in the road. Unwinking eyes that began to swim before Marks's gaze as the grip around his throat choked off the air from his lungs and the blood from his brain.

Within seconds his knees were sagging and the beat of his hands at those iron-hard wrists was weak and utterly futile. The giggle of the half-dressed woman and the hiss of the prancing boy were the last things he heard while consciousness lasted.

And those staring unmatched eyes, burning up implacably into his brain, were the last things he saw before he plunged into oblivion.

Chapter Twelve

Anne Ashby, the only female director of The Guardians, was suitably dressed and equipped for her vigil near the Glasgow house in which Fergus Trayle was staying.

Her dark grey long-sleeved blouse and slacks

melted into the background of the city dusk, and the light-weight black hip-length jacket she also wore saved the outfit from looking too conspicuous should she be noticed loitering.

A sleeve of the jacket concealed her one item of equipment. This was an article of jewelry, her only such article apart from a fob-watch in the front pocket of her slacks.

It was a flat silver bangle encircling her right wrist. Of ancient workmanship, it was known as a Sybil's Annulus or Seer's Circlet. Made from silver ore which had been smelted when the moon was in Cancer, it conformed in that particular and in every detail of its design with the requirements of its occult purpose.

An unbroken band two inches in width, it had been engraved with the vibrationary Words of Power ruling past, present and future, and also with several symbols. The Tree of Knowledge was flanked by the esoteric symbols of Opening the Eye and Opening the Mouth. Beside the Opening the Eye symbol was that of the Astral Sea. The center symbol was that of the Tree of Life, and at the extremities of the engraved design were the sygils of the Mansions of the Moon, with above them the Silver Vessel of Night and the Golden Vessel of Day.

If worn constantly the Annulus was supposed to give its wearer heightened perception and intuition. Worn on the right wrist, as Anne was now wearing it, it was by tradition supposed to give psychic insight into the future, and on the left wrist insight into the past.

These results were not automatic. The Annulus could only heighten psychic sensitivity already possessed by the wearer; even then the enlightening inspiration could be delayed.

But, as an amulet, Anne Ashby often wore it when on an assignment against malefic occultism.

The Annulus aided another of Anne's special faculties—that of making her mind entirely unreadable by telepathy.

When keeping vigil on a man with the powers credited to Fergus Trayle, such a mental protection might be invaluable. And tonight it was to prove so.

Because the Trayle house was at the end of a row of houses, where two streets intersected, and had a tradesmen's alley at the rear, it was easy to keep watch on both the front and back entrances.

Not long after darkness had fallen, a number of people, singly and in twos and threes, called at Cosmo Trayle's house via the tradesmen's alley and were admitted.

That the callers were not tradesmen was obvious. Tradesmen would not call at night, nor in the smart clothes these visitors were wearing. Nor would tradesmen arrive on foot.

Anne was surprised, but suspected that they had come most of the way by car and had parked their cars at a little distance from the house in order to avoid attracting attention.

The alley at the rear of the house had, as Steven Kane had ascertained earlier, a series of inset doors which admitted visitors into the small back gardens. A garden path led to the actual back door of the house.

From her vantage point Anne saw none of the visitors use a key, so evidently the tradesmen's door into the back garden was not locked. The callers merely twisted the door handle and walked straight in. Presumably when they reached the back door of the house they knocked or rang for admittance.

What was the purpose of their visit—a bridge party? Anne smiled sardonically at the idea. From what she had heard, the elegant Cosmo Trayle might have such a social interest, but his uncouth brother was not likely to share it. Besides, there had been too many callers for an ordinary bridge party.

What kind of party, then? A drinking party? Again Anne smiled. Had they come on foot because they did not expect to be in a fit condition to drive home? No. 'Don't drink and drive' was too considerate a precept to appeal to the Trayles and their friends.

But were these back-door visitors friends of the Trayles? Mightn't they be victims or prospective victims? Anne did not think so. In her experience predators liked to outnumber their victims, to take them one at a time, not face them *en masse*. They also liked to make it difficult for their victims to confer together and compare notes.

So it seemed most probable that tonight's callers, even if not personal friends of the Trayles, were associates of some kind. Fellow conspirators, fellow occultists, fellow initiates . . .

The thought gave Anne Ashby an idea that made her slender, sinuous body tense like that of a cat newly aroused from sleep and ready for its nightly hunt.

She would not mention the idea to Steven Kane—until afterwards. Then he would have no chance to veto it.

She was a director of The Guardians, with a director's right of personal initiative. Her anticipatory smile became subtle. In some ways she was a very privileged director, more privileged than any of them.

All the same, she would not invite a clash of wills with Steven Kane, not even over the telephone. Professor Kane was The Guardians' principal. He would have the right to remind her of that. But if he were presented with a *fait accompli*, nothing he might say or do could make any difference.

Anne, as well as Kane himself, was very much aware of the hidden antagonism which existed between them—an antagonism which was, however, in no way allowed to interfere with their work. She knew that Kane was both intrigued and vaguely repelled by her—drawn by her sexuality, repelled by her suspected association with Gideon Cross, The Guardians' founder. If Anne had chosen to do so, she might have explained that association, but she did not choose to. In some way she got a certain satisfaction—perhaps a purely feminine one—in knowing that Steven Kane's thoughts were often occupied with her, and not on a professional basis.

Now, after waiting to see if any further visitors were coming to the Trayle house, Anne eased herself out of her dark corner and strolled casually across the intersecting, deserted sidestreet.

With her hands in her side pockets, she made unhurriedly for the tradesmen's alley and the rear entrance of the Trayle house.

Fergus Trayle's party, whatever its motive and nature, was about to have a gate-crasher.

Anne moved softly. The high wall in which the alley's rear door was set was surmounted with a jagged line of broken glass cemented into place as a deterrent to intruders—which seemed rather comic when a twist of her hand on the door-knob gave her instant access to the garden.

As might have been expected of Cosmo Trayle's domestic environment, the garden was fastidiously neat, with a straight cement path leading between impeccable flowerbeds.

The only sign of life was a pair of green eyes watching her from the top of the wall at the side. But there was too much of the feline in Anne Ashby's own nature for a common garden cat to bother her. With the gaze of those inscrutable eyes following her, she approached the shadowed back door of the house.

The window beside it was darkened by a lowered blind. Her exploring fingers found a bell-push in the center of the door and gently pressed it.

The ringing inside the house was audible to her, but only just.

There was no immediate response to the ring. No doubt, she thought, the party had already started . . . without this unexpected and self-invited guest.

So she waited patiently for someone to drag himself away from it. She already knew that there were no servants in the house.

Abruptly the door swung open. Light at the far end of a long passage cast into dark silhouette a large head craning around its edge.

Some of the light from that distant source illuminated Anne's face and figure. A bearded chin jutted around the door-edge and a mouth opened to fan a malodorous breath into her face.

"Who the . . . devil are you?" a gruff voice inquired crudely.

With a disarming smile, Anne Ashby for a moment held up her right hand where the light would fall on it—with her index and little fingers raised and her other fingers and thumb bent down.

It was the sign of the 'horned hand,' a sign of introduction and recognition between witchcraft initiates. As soon as the bearded man had had time to assimilate it, Anne lowered her hand.

"Mmmm . . ." he growled. But he did so musingly. His mind was obviously not fully on the sign, but was apparently preoccupied with the attraction of her face and figure, so conveniently illuminated for his inspection.

She could almost feel his scrutiny following every contour of her body.

But his first word expressed no opinion—merely a question. "So . . . ?"

"The party," she said. "Don't you welcome those who . . . belong?"

Again a scrutiny she could almost feel as well as observe, then a gruff, non-committal invitation.

"You can come in."

Even an uninformed woman would have needed courage to step past the bearded man into the house, and Anne Ashby had an experienced person's comprehension regarding the kind of circle into which she was venturing. Also, three working directors of The Guardians had come to Scotland because of the possibility that Fergus Trayle was morally capable of making his fatal prophesy come true; that he was capable of murder.

But no hint of trepidation showed in Anne's smooth face. She unhesitatingly stepped inside.

She was just clear of the open door when it slammed quickly shut behind her. And immediately afterwards she heard bolts being driven home. The door had not been bolted before her arrival. In spite of her outward composure Anne was aware of an uncomfortable feeling at the base of her spine and along the back of her neck, where the soft dark hair curled.

A heavy hand fell on her shoulder from behind and the sour breath was now an invisible cloud just above her head.

"Go straight on," the husky voice ordered.

Anne was under no illusions as to why she had been asked inside. She knew or suspected too much to be sent away unquestioned, before her motive for coming to the house had been investigated. If she could satisfy Fergus Trayle of her sympathy with the kind of things he did, she had a chance of leaving the house unharmed.

But if not . . . those bolts had not been shot for nothing. She would be much less of a menace inside the house than roaming at large outside and able to talk.

The treatment she would receive here depended on whether she could convince Trayle that, in the terminology of initiates, she 'belonged.'

She was escorted to the end of the long passage, where an arm reached past her to open a half-open door to its full extent. It was from this room that the light had fanned out.

"Inside," the Hermit of Black Loch said curtly.

With the poise of a professional model, Anne Ashby sauntered into the room.

It was larger than she had expected—or perhaps it looked larger because of its furnishings, unusual in a private house.

At the far end was a raised platform and facing it were rows of chairs arranged in two blocks, divided by a central aisle. It might have been a private chapel or lecture hall—except for the subject of the three paintings adorning the walls.

Above the platform, on the end wall, was a large oil which she recognised as a copy of a famous one by Hieronymus Bosch, Flemish painter of mediaeval witchcraft. It was a vividly depicted scene of dementia. On the side walls were similar but smaller paintings in imitation, respectively, of works by Adrianus Hubertus and Breughel the Elder. They, too, horrifically concerned witchcraft.

It said much for the power of these paintings that Anne caught much of their detail before her eyes focused on the living people gathered in the room.

Most were seated on the audience chairs, but had turned to stare at her inquisitively. In the cleared space near the door two men and a woman were standing as ushers.

The woman, though not very young, was wearing a mini-skirt. But this, Anne realized, had a specific function—to make visible the decorative garter she was wearing above her left knee. The garter was made of green snakeskin on a backing of blue silk, and was fastened with a gold or gilt buckle. Anne recognized it as a ritual garter, indicating the wearer's rank in a witch community.

Anne had seen and sensed depravity in human faces before. But, given the power to discern it, perhaps only a woman of her strange antecedents would not have been overwhelmed by the psychic gust of evil which swept over her from the assembled watchers.

Now along the aisle came someone who at first glance might have been mistaken for a boy, and whom Anne had assumed to be a boy when he had arrived in the dimly-lit alley, walking between two adults. But her lancing scrutiny now told her that the diminutive figure approaching was, in fact, a dwarf.

The discovery did not surprise her.

Early in Highland history it had been traditional for a clan chief to have an attendant dwarf, probably descended from the short-statured, broad-shouldered Picts. These clan dwarfs had notoriously been possessed of great physical strength and, according to legend, of occult interests.

The dwarf now sidling past the ushers to get a closer look at the unexpected visitor might easily have filled that historical role, Anne thought. And if Fergus Trayle had delusions of grandeur, it was understandable that he and his undersized guest should gravitate to each other, presuming that the dwarf shared the Hermit's occult inclinations.

Fergus had followed Anne into the room and closed the door. Seeing the direction of her gaze, he gave a grin.

"That's our *Du-Sith*," he said, eyeing her keenly.

"Your Black Elf!" she interpreted aloud. Then, to the dwarf, she said coolly: "How do you do?"

Grinning up at her from under his beetling brows like the elf after which he had been named, he twisted her greeting into a question and replied with a leering innuendo:

"If you're stayin', mah beauty, I'll be doin' fine!"

Fergus Trayle scowled down at him. "Don't overreach yourself, little man," he said malevolently. "This lady is *my* guest. So far. And before we make any more introductions, let's hear from her."

The dwarf insisted eagerly: "She'd make a fine altar!"

Anne smiled, as if she had received a normal compliment. "Thank you."

The bearded man scowled again. "The important thing," he said, his glare paralyzing even the dwarf, "is to find out what the lady really has in her mind!"

Grasping Anne by an arm, he urged her into the aisle and towards the platform. On the faces that turned to follow their progress there was but one expression, that of keen anticipation.

Obviously her arrival had held up the planned program, but whatever that program might be, the people in this particular congregation were evidently more than willing to defer it until after the interrogation of the intruder.

And none was more willing than the so-called 'Du-Sith,' the Black Elf. Roused from his temporary cowed posture, he turned and trotted after the Hermit and Anne.

Never more than now, Anne thought, did she need an unreadable mind.

Chapter Thirteen

Lionel Marks, his plump face mask-like, drove his MG southwards from the Rathlaw estate and did not stop until he reached an R.A.C. roadside telephone booth. There he made a trunk call to Steven Kane's hotel in Glasgow.

"Sorry to be late," he said, when Kane answered. "But I followed Donald and Fiona all the way home to the Castle, to make sure they arrived safely—had no chance to phone you again on the way there."

"Where are you now?" asked Steven.

"About eighteen miles from Rathlaw Castle—"

Kane's voice was approving. "You were wise not to lose contact with them, Lionel. I'll admit I was beginning to get worried, wondering why you hadn't phoned. Nothing more to report since your last call?"

"No. Only their safe arrival home. The run was quite without incident."

"Did you call at the Castle?"

"No," said Marks. "Once I'd crossed the boundary of the estate I switched off my lights and followed their car till I saw it enter the Castle gates. Then I turned back to find a phone—I thought it better to call you from a box before going back to the Castle and begging a bed. That's if you want me to stay there, of course."

"Yes," said Kane promptly. "Go to the Castle as if you've just arrived. Say you expected to find me there; they can't do more than offer to put you up for the night. Don't mention seeing Donald and the girl in Aberdeen—but you'd better stay as close to them as you can until after the wedding." He broke off, then added: "Have you caught a cold, Lionel?"

"No. Why?"

"I thought your voice sounded different—flat, not very clear . . ."

"I'm tired," said Marks. "I've had a pretty tiring day."

"Of course," said Kane. He went on: "By the way, Anne seems to have disappeared. I went to relieve her of the watch on Trayle's place, but there's no sign of her."

"Oh," said Marks.

126

Kane said, with a touch of irritation as well as surprise: "You don't seem very worried—"

"Anne can take care of herself," said Marks. "She's probably followed Fergus somewhere."

"Maybe—but I'm anxious, just the same. But I'll deal with things this end—you get back to the Castle and keep an eye on young Donald." He added: "We can't afford to take any chances in that direction, Lionel."

"Well, he's safe enough at the moment—"

"You go back there." Kane spoke with decisiveness. "Find a chance to phone me tomorrow. If neither Anne nor myself should be here, at the hotel, leave a message with the switchboard operator. Now I know young Rathlaw's safe at the Castle I can start a more thorough hunt for Anne. Goodnight, Lionel."

"Goodnight," replied Marks, and rang off.

For a moment Kane stood with the receiver in his hand, staring down at it with a puzzled frown. There had been something in Marks's voice which had vaguely worried him—almost a note of indifference. Then he shrugged, replacing the handset with a wry smile. No doubt Marks was, as he had said, tired. On the other hand, it was unlike the normally ebullient little man to sound so lackadasical; even in his more harrassed moments he could usually find time for a quip or a joke—often at Kane's expense.

Steven Kane's expression was still thoughtful when, some minutes later, he left his room and went quickly out of the hotel.

After Marks had replaced the telephone receiver he stood for a moment quite motionless, staring at the wall of the telephone box. Then, with an unusual slow deliberation, he dialed another number.

When he was connected Marks spoke with the same slow deliberation.

"I have just reported Rathlaw's safe arrival to Steven Kane," he said in a peculiarly flat tone.

"And what has Steven Kane reported to you?"

Obediently Marks replied: "Kane has reported that our fellow director, Anne Ashby, is missing."

There was a soft chuckle in the earpiece. "Don't you worry about that, Mr. Marks. Just tell me what Mr. Kane wants you to do now."

"I'm to go back to Rathlaw Castle to keep an eye on Donald."

"Excellent. You do that. And no doubt you're expected to telephone another report to Mr. Kane tomorrow—or rather, later today. It's well past two A.M."

"Yes. After a night's sleep I have to find a chance to phone him."

"Before you do so, telephone me again. I may have something for you to include in your report to Mr. Kane. You understand that?"

"Yes. I understand."

"Then go and get your night's rest at the Castle. Your . . . guardianship of Donald Rathlaw will soon be ended."

Marks stood listening without comment until he heard the connection cut off. Then he stepped out of the R.A.C. box and returned to his car. A minute later he was driving towards Rathlaw Castle.

Lionel Marks, ex-private agent, was the least profound of The Guardians' directors. He could not match the insight and erudition of Steven Kane and Father John Dyball.

And he lacked Anne Ashby's ability to keep her mind blank under hypnosis.

Before Marks had telephoned his two reports, Anne Ashby's resistance to hypnotic interrogation had been put to a severe test.

From a mental void she slowly emerged to find herself seated on a high-backed chair in the center of the platform in the Trayles' meeting-room.

Fergus Trayle was standing over her, his gaze still intent on her face. Also on the platform, watching her, were the gartered woman and the dwarf. The dwarf still leered at Anne, but with more cause now than before.

Anne knew that she had been searched, and in the only way that had been thorough enough for these people. She had been stripped. Her clothes were lying in a heap beside her chair. With them was her silver annulus.

She treated her unclad state with the unconcern of a woman aware that her superb figure could stand inspection. But she hoped that her unconcern would be interpreted as the indifference of one who had taken part in many a Sabbat. She hoped also that nobody would notice that the insides of her palms were slightly damp with sweat and was thankful they could not see how her dry tongue clung to the roof of her mouth.

"I telt ye she'd make a fine altar!" the dwarf said exultantly.

"Or Queen of the Sabbat," Fergus Trayle mused. "If I didn't have another in view. But our . . . guest interests me exceedingly. She has a very peculiar power. Never before have I found a mind remain totally blank under my probing. And it wasn't because of any amulet. Her only one was that annulus —and it made no difference when we took it off."

Anne spoke for the first time since coming out of the void.

Urbanely she drawled: "Perhaps you'll give me my annulus back—now that you've satisfied yourselves I am one of you. I value that trinket—"

"No doubt you do," Fergus Trayle agreed, still frowning uncertainly. "If you're indeed one of us, you must rank very high. But there are adepts of the Right Hand Path, too. If you are one of *our* kind, why should you make your mind blank? Why should you keep secrets from friends?"

Anne retorted: "I don't keep secrets from friends. But friends *ask* me anything they want to know. They don't try to drag it out of my mind. I've advanced too far on the Path to tolerate that kind of insult. You can take it as proof of my friendly intentions that I merely made my mind blank. Had I wished, I could have given you absurd fantasies to read there. I could have deliberately confused you."

Fergus Trayle grinned with contempt. "Had you tried that, I'd have spotted the trick right away. Only a complete blank could serve you against me. But here—" He stooped and snatched something up from beside her heap of clothing "—here's that annulus of yours. You're welcome to it. If it tells you anything of the future it must tell you what your fate will be if you cross me."

Frowning, he went on slowly: "That's why I'm inclined to think you're genuine. Only a rash fool would cross swords with me—and you're no fool. You know things; you took the risk of coming here because you didn't fear the outcome. That suggests—"

Somewhere in the house a telephone rang. Fergus

said gruffly to Anne: "You can put your clothes on now. But stay there!" He turned, went down the platform steps and strode from the room.

Disdainfully ignoring the rapt attention of the dwarf, Anne dressed. Then she seated herself again and lounged back in the chair, returning the stares of the depraved congregation.

Ten minutes passed before Fergus came back. And when he sent the door crashing open and came walking rapidly down the aisle to the platform, there was a glare of sheer devilry in his unmatched eyes.

Dispensing with the steps, he jumped up on to the platform and glowered at close range into Anne's face.

"So . . . Anne Ashby!" he jibed. "You came here with friendly intentions, eh? My brother has just informed me that a colleague of yours has directly contradicted you. Unfortunately for that colleague —and for you—he can't blank out his mind as you can yours. Nor is he resistent to hypnosis. And it seems that you are one of three meddlers who came to Scotland in the hope of saving young Donald Rathlaw from the doom that is coming to him. Which makes your visit here tonight very . . . friendly, eh?"

He straightened up, but still glared at her.

"There are ways of making even you talk—if it were necessary now. Physical ways . . ."

Anne cut in: "As well as making my mind a blank against questions, I can make myself unconscious against torture. So that would gain you nothing."

"It would give me the satisfaction of teaching you a lesson, because it would leave you in pain when you recovered consciousness, wouldn't it! But I've already said that there's no need for me to make you talk. Your colleague, Marks, has told us all we need to know. Which means we shall be getting away from here almost immediately—and taking you with us."

He turned to speak to the dwarf: "Wee fellow, you were right when you said she'd make a fine altar. You shall see just how fine if you make a good job of something I want you to do. First, take that thing off her wrist again."

His eyes alight with gleeful anticipation, the broad-shouldered dwarf roughly snatched the silver annulus from Anne's wrist and handed it back to Trayle.

Fergus Trayle gripped Anne brutally by one shoulder, then addressed the congregation:

"My friends," he said, "it behooves us to leave here almost at once. This time you will leave by the front door. And you'll be able to do so without trouble, because our little *Du-Sith* will be taking care of the last of the meddlers. Just wait till I give you the word, then go out by the front door and return to your cars. I'll be leaving at the same time, in the car my brother left in the garage, in case I should need it. And I'll be taking this . . . lady with me."

Those seated waited relaxed for his permission to leave. Trayle brought a far-from-clean handkerchief from his pocket and unceremoniously gagged Anne. Then, gripping her shoulder again, he stooped and whispered urgently into the dwarf's ear, at the same time giving him the annulus.

Before straightening up, he said audibly: "Before I leave I'll watch you for a sign that he's taking the bait. Quite sure you don't need any help? That you can handle him?"

The dwarf, grinning, squared his broad shoulders and flexed his thick arms.

"Have I ever failed yet?" he challenged.

"Go on then, I'll watch you from the kitchen."

Trayle dragged Anne with him. In the kitchen at the back of the house, he raised the blind a little so that he could watch the dark garden and its exit door in the high boundary wall.

With the annulus clutched in a large paw, the dwarf trotted off along the path to that door opening on to the tradesmen's alley.

It was inevitable that Steven Kane, in his search for Anne, should come to the alley at the rear of the Trayle's house.

When he arrived, it was deserted and quiet. At the end nearest to the house the passage was at it gloomiest, since the street lamp that provided its only illumination was at the distant opposite end. But that glow was sufficient to cause a reflected gleam from some metallic object lying in the dirt near the wall.

Kane went closer, stepping cautiously, and with a wary glance for the half-open door. It took him only a second to recognise the object as Anne Ashby's silver annulus.

As he stooped to pick it up, something came off the top of the wall above him. It had been lying there, flat against the brickwork and seemingly impervious to the glass shards cemented into the coping. Kane never saw it. As he was reaching for the annulus, the dark shape of spread-eagled arms and legs launched itself down on to his bent back. The weight that hit Kane in the small of the back was relatively light. But the strength in the short legs that gripped him around the waist and in the predatory arms that wound around his neck was much greater than that of most men of normal size.

Kane staggered under it and fell flat on his face.

He could not wriggle free. A pair of large and powerful hands gripped his throat. Thick fingers dug into his jugular and windpipe.

Kane would not have known if a hundred people had been leaving the front door of the house.

With his eyes hot and already bulging, with his starved lungs an agony in his chest, he knew that in a matter of seconds this double throttling grip would make him a dead man.

His heart was fibrillating to its last feeble beats.

Chapter Fourteen

Face shining pinkly from his bath, Donald Rathlaw entered the bridal suite's bedroom.

He was in a hotel in Dunoon, on the west of the Firth of Clyde.

That morning he and Fiona had been married, the ceremony taking place in the Rathlaw Castle chapel and conducted by the Laird's own chaplain. At the subsequent reception there had been one extra guest —Lionel Marks.

A couple of hours after Donald and Fiona had returned from their trip to Aberdeen, Marks had arrived at the Castle and informed Sir Alastair that he had been deputized by Steven Kane to guard the young couple.

Donald had not been keen to have a third party

following him and Fiona around, but to allay his father's anxiety he had good-naturedly agreed. To Fiona he had humorously explained that it was not only heads of State who had bodyguards, but prospective heads of a clan—though in this case, he had assured her, it was a mere formality.

As a staunch patriot, Donald had decided immediately upon becoming engaged that the honeymoon should be spent in that country which, in his opinion, had no equal. The specific place selected, the holiday resort of Dunoon, was not only a convenient center for car and steamer trips to other places of interest, but provided golf, tennis, angling, yachting and a Continental casino. And its hotels were quite good.

Donald was in such high spirits that he even agreed to allow Lionel Marks to watch over himself and Fiona during the honeymoon—but from a discreet distance. So Marks was doing so, near their suite but from his own room on the same corridor.

No thought of their self-elected guardian was in Donald's mind at the moment. In a shimmering new silk dressing-gown which had been one of his wedding presents, he strolled into the bridal bedroom, to find Fiona already in the big double bed, her hair a startling red against the white pillow.

She was half sitting up, and her hair was not her only striking feature. No one older or less lovely could have done such justice to the bridal nightdress she was wearing. It was a smoky green, diaphanously unsubstantial, too revealing in design to allow Donald any doubt that he was among the luckiest men in the world.

Fiona met his ardent gaze, flushing slightly and smiling as he approached the bed. He sat down on the edge, put an arm around her bare shoulders, tilted

her chin and kissed her passionately. At first she reacted instinctively in kind. Then, as he leaned over
her with both arms around her, he felt her body suddenly stiffen.

She turned her face away. The flush faded from
her cheeks until they were cold and pale. Suddenly
Donald felt foolish, as though embracing an inert
dummy.

"Hey—Mrs. Rathlaw!" he chided gently. "What's
this." He reached up to turn her face back towards
him, but her throat muscles tautened in resistance.

"Fiona!" he exclaimed, mildly protesting. "Not
now, darling. This is what we've been waiting
for . . ."

Now she moved. She clutched at the bedclothes to
drag them up over the revealing top of the nightdress. But still she did not look at him.

Donald's face reddened with humiliation.

"Fiona," he chided again, still gently. "This is our
wedding night. What have I done to upset you?"

Holding the bedclothes tightly to her chest, Fiona
now returned his gaze. Her expression was icily remote. It was almost one of dislike. And she had not
spoken a word since he had come into the bedroom.

The sparkle died out of Donald's eyes. As a bridegroom he felt foolish, insulted, and he was beginning
to feel angry. Yet she had been vivacious and talka-
tive, gay and laughing on the drive down from
Rathlaw.

Ironically he asked: "D'you want to read or something?"

"No," she said curtly.

"Well, when you put that sort of nightdress on,
did you expect *me* to want to read?"

136

She frowned. Then, sullenly she murmured: "I'm sorry, Donald. I just want to be left alone."

His anger heightened. "Oh! You came on a honeymoon and you put on that tantalizing nightdress—just because you wanted to be left alone? I should have realized it, of course. Forgive my denseness."

She turned away and laid her head on the pillow. In the same cold tone she muttered: "Don't be sarcastic, please. I'm tired. I want to sleep."

"You want to sleep? Literally to sleep, eh? Not metaphorically but literally. You're sure you wouldn't like a room to yourself?"

She ignored him. Frustrated, Donald grasped her shoulders and twisted her around.

"Fiona," he demanded. "What's all this about? I know you drew a line before—but now . . . now we're married." Bitter words burst from him. "Don't tell me it was just the ceremony you wanted—" He added: "Or the married status?"

She scowled with derisive distaste. "Well, did you think I had a craving for you as a man?"

"What?" He stared at her in shocked horror. All the ardor in him evaporated. He removed his hands from her shoulders.

"My God!" he breathed. "I've heard of things like this . . . but a man never dreams it can happen to *him*. It's too . . . incredible." Disbelief made him lean towards her again. "Fiona! Tell me you don't mean it. You're just—nervous, perhaps . . ." He was almost pleading with her now.

For a brief second or two a mental struggle showed in her face and eyes. One of her hands reached out for him, the hand wearing a shining new wedding-ring.

"Donald!" she whimpered. "What have I said?"

Baffled, he peered keenly into her face, then took hold of her abruptly and held her close to him.

"You're not yourself, Fiona," he whispered. "No quarrels tonight, dearest. Not tonight of all nights. You know how much you mean to me."

Her voice came harshly, in crude and brittle rebuff.

"Spare me that sentimentality, will you! Just leave me alone—" And with surprising strength she pushed him away.

Donald simply did not know what to do. It was as if some alien, hostile personality had taken possession of her. As if her true nature, after one or two feeble attempts to assert itself, had finally been submerged.

And then the terrifying thought flooded into his mind.

"My God!" he blurted. "That curse! That damned curse!"

He stared at her dazedly as she pushed the bedclothes aside and swung her legs out of bed. The nightdress, specially designed to be provocative, was slit up one side and held together by tied ribbons at hip, waist and armpit. But the sight of his bride's sleek white thighs as she stood roused no passion in Donald now. He watched dully as she walked around the bed.

When she crossed, barefooted, to the front door, he swung after her, jealously outraged.

"Fiona! You can't go out into the public corridor dressed like that! Why d'you want to go out there, anyway?"

Again she ignored him. Her fingers were on the door handle when he overtook her and gripped her arm.

"Fiona—are you mad? Going out like that? I won't let you!"

He tried to turn her around, but she dug her bare feet into the carpet, wrenched her arm away and tugged at the knob. She almost spat at him over her shoulder:

"Let me go, you fool! I'm not staying here—"

"Then get dressed, for God's sake! You can't—"

But she did go out. She got the door unfastened. A sudden violent thrust of her elbow against his chest caught him by surprise. When he had recovered his balance the door had slammed shut in his face.

He was about to follow her when one of his slippers fell off. In frantic haste he rammed his foot back into it and reached for the door.

In the corridor he flashed glances both ways. He saw Fiona ahead of him, walking towards the lifts and the stairwell, brazenly indifferent to her near-nakedness.

Before he had moved a couple of yards she had a finger on the lift button. He was still four yards short of her when the rising lift stopped and its doors slid open to admit her. He sprinted.

When he skidded to a stop the lift-doors too had slammed shut in his face. He knew that she was on her way down to ground level, with the intention of leaving the hotel altogether.

What the devil was wrong, he asked himself desperately. Had she gone completely out of her mind?

There was no time to wait for the lift to return. Impatiently he dashed into the stair-well which spiralled round the lift-shaft. In his headlong rush down the stairs he lost both slippers but careless of discomfort and appearances, he continued to the bottom.

When he emerged into the hotel reception lounge he had a passing glimpse of the night reception clerk just aroused from a doze—and a back view of Fiona passing out through the swinging glass doors to the street.

Donald, his dressing-gown and pyjama legs flapping, hurled himself across the lounge and out through the doors to the entrance steps. Fiona was walking steadily, like a sleepwalker, along the pave-ent. At that hour no other pedestrian was in sight, but fifty yards from the hotel entrance a car was parked. It now began crawling along the curbside towards Fiona.

It reached her before Donald could do so. A rear door opened and she was pulled inside, and even in his frantic fear and astonishment Donald noticed that she made no resistance. The car door closed but the car did not drive away.

It continued to crawl in the same direction until it was level with Donald. Panting, he leaned down towards the opening front door of the vehicle.

Sticking his head inside he demanded furiously: "What the devil's going on? That's my wife you've just—"

The words were abruptly guillotined. Something hard and heavy, wielded by someone in the rear seat, made a violent impact with the back of Donald's neck. Instantly he blacked out, slumping forward into the car.

His unconscious body was dragged inside and the car door closed.

Now the car drove away quickly, into the night.

Back in the hotel Lionel Marks rose from the chair on which he had been sitting, watching the corridor through an inch-wide aperture of his partly-opened door.

He had seen Fiona go by and enter the lift. He had seen Donald rush after her and into the stair-well. But the spectacle had caused him only a mild interest, as though he had been watching some not-very-interesting film.

Standing up, he gave an indifferent shrug, yawned, and moved away from the door. He locked it, almost absently, then crossed towards the bed.

His brief vigil was over. His job was done. Now he could get some sleep.

Marks awoke to an insistent knocking on the door of his room. Blearily he opened his eyes; muzzily he called out:

"Whozzat?"

"Steven Kane. Open up!" There was urgency in the voice.

Marks slid slowly out of bed and, still clad in his pyjamas, crossed the carpeted floor. He yawned again, running his fingers through his sparse, untidy hair.

"Hurry up! What the devil's keeping you?" The knocking came again, louder and more prolonged.

"All right, all right," grumbled Marks. "I'm coming. By my life, this is a fine way to wake a man—"

He fumbled with the key and turned it. The door opened almost violently, then Steven Kane strode past his surprised colleague into the room. In the middle of the carpet he turned and faced Marks.

His face was grimly set and his dark eyes held a hostile gleam. Marks put out a protesting hand.

"Not before the coffee and marmalade, please!" he begged.

"Cut out the humor," snapped Kane. "I fancy some explanations are due from you, my friend!"

Marks returned his chill gaze with bewilderment, and again ran stubby fingers through his sleep-tousled hair.

"What time is it?" he asked vaguely.

With taut irony Kane said: "You might well ask. It's past eight o'clock—and you're still in bed. Weren't you supposed to be keeping watch on young Donald Rathlaw and his bride?"

"But . . ."

"I realize that you have to get some sleep some time. But it does seem a little inappropriate for you to be blissfully sleeping—when the couple you're supposed to be guarding have disappeared."

"Disappeared!" Lionel Marks came to full alertness with a jolt. "You're talking like a fool. I saw them both safely into their room last night—"

"And the reception clerk saw them go out again. After midnight. What's more they were both in their nightclothes—"

Marks's jaw dropped and he stared at his companion owlishly. "In their *night-clothes?* But—"

"But me no buts," said Kane. "What were *you* doing when Fiona went out of the hotel in her nightdress and Donald ran after her in his pyjamas? That's what I want to know—and I want an answer, fast!"

Marks's stomach seemed to drop away from inside him; he put out a hand and groped for a chair. He gasped: "But they couldn't have! I was watching all the time! I sat just inside the door and I never took my eyes off that corridor—"

"You're sure?"

"Well . . ." Marks ran a hand over his forehead.

"There was a minute or two when I felt sleepy. But only for a minute—I don't even remember closing my eyes. And if I had done, I'd have heard them—"

Kane's glance flickered around the room, and when he spoke again his tone had subtly altered. The anger had gone out of it. He put a hand on Marks's shoulder and pushed him down gently into the chair behind him. He said quietly:

"Sit down, Lionel. And listen carefully. You say you were sitting against the door looking into the corridor—do you remember getting up from the chair and going to bed?"

"No—no. Come to think of it, I don't remember much at all except putting the chair against the door and sitting down. But I'm sure I didn't go to sleep, Steven!" There was a note almost of pleading in the other man's voice.

Kane gripped his shoulder reassuringly. "I believe you, Lionel. But there are . . . influences at work here. There isn't time for me to ask you a lot of questions. especially when it's highly probable you couldn't give me any logical answers. So I'll ask you just one—"

He paused, then leaned forward, thrusting his strong face almost into Marks's own. His voice was crisp and decisive. He said:

"Have you any objection to my putting you under hypnosis?"

Chapter Fifteen

Lionel Marks looked startled.

"In the name of Solomon—why? Anyway, d'you think you could do it?"

Kane said, still in that tautly quiet voice: "I've a suspicion, Lionel, that you're not impervious to hypnosis."

Marks shrugged. "I suppose you've some reason for suggesting it. So—if it'll make you happy—you're welcome to try. But be careful! Did I ever tell you the story about the hypnotist and the stevedore? It seems this hypnotist told him to—"

"I've heard it," said Kane patiently. "Now sit back and keep quiet."

He wasted no further time. Because the curtains had not yet been drawn back, the room was only dimly lit by the summer daylight filtering through them. He switched on the bedside lamp and swivelled it so that it shone directly into Marks's eyes. Marks blinked, wanting to turn away, but conscious of the grimly forbidding expression on his companion's face.

From his breast pocket Kane brought a silver-topped ball-point pen and held its silver cap towards Marks.

"Keep watching this!" he said.

He kept the silver cap in the beam of light shining

into Marks's face, but high enough to make it necessary for Marks to strain his eyes upwards to keep it in view. He kept moving the pen slowly and rhythmically . . .

The rapidity with which Marks went under supported Kane's suspicion that he had been hypnotized before—and very recently. A subject who had been under hypnotic control was always easier to hypnotize on subsequent occasions.

It was half-an-hour later when Kane snapped his colleague out of his deep trance.

Marks grinned up at him.

"Told you so. You can't do it, eh? I'm a tougher nut than you expected."

Kane switched off the lamp and said bluntly: "You offered as much resistance as anyone else who has been hypnotized before. None."

Marks sat upright, surprised and outraged. "By the Lord Harry, Steven, you're not trying to tell me—"

"I'm not *trying* to tell you anything. I am telling you. You've been hypnotized—but you remember no more of it then you remember being hypnotized by Cosmo Trayle on the night you drove up to Rathlaw from Aberdeen—"

Marks's jaw dropped. Standing there in his rumpled pyjamas, his thinning hair on end, his eyes opened like those of a startled fox, the lower bridgework of his shining dentures gleaming pinkly, he presented a ludicrous figure. At any other time Kane would have laughed. Now he said:

"You don't remember anything about that, either? About meeting Cosmo Trayle?"

"N-no . . ."

"In twenty-five minutes under hypnosis, Lionel, you've told me things I'd never have learned by ordinary questioning. About the incident near Rathlaw, when you were stopped by Cosmo Trayle and the Erskines. Trayle had suppressed that incident entirely from your conscious memory."

"You mean I was hypnotized by Trayle without knowing it?" Marks demanded incredulously.

Kane nodded. "You were trapped and turned loose to obey instructions. One was to telephone me, giving your report, the other was to relate to Cosmo Trayle anything and everything I had told you. You were to say nothing to me about what you had told him. You were to keep in touch with Trayle through a telephone number supplied by him. You were to continue your watch on Donald and Fiona but do nothing if you saw that they were in danger—"

"It should happen to me!" Marks groaned. Then he stood up, went across the room and drew the window curtains back, letting in a dazzling flood of daylight. The action seemed to clarify his mind for when he turned back to Kane again his voice was brisker and his eyes were normally alert.

"So what do we do now?" he asked.

Kane said: "Get washed, shaved and dressed. While you're doing that, I'll give you more of the picture."

"But if I'm still under Cosmo Trayle's influence to report everything back to him, wouldn't that be dangerous?" Marks protested.

Kane's expression was reassuring. "Not now. I've removed Trayle's post-hypnotic control over you." He added: "Don't feel too badly about it, Lionel. If anyone is to blame, it's me—I should have been prepared for something like this, knowing Cosmo's powers."

While Marks was washing and shaving Kane said:

146

"I told you that Anne had disappeared, didn't I? She's still missing. I'm afraid she must have been trapped by Fergus—no doubt as a result of information extracted from you and passed to him by Cosmo."

Marks winced, and not because he had cut himself. His plump face was unhappy. "All my fault," he mourned. "If they harm her—"

"Let's leave probabilities and possibilities out of it for the moment," said Kane. "I haven't told you yet that I was nearly choked to death by some damned dwarf—"

Marks stared at him. "A dwarf?"

"And as strong as an ox. God knows how I got away—he had a grip on my throat like a bulldog. Nothing but the good old Polynesian *vagus coup* would dispose of him—and as you know, that's fatal." Kane's field work in primitive anthropology had given him some very esoteric items of knowledge.

He went on: "I guessed that his attack on me had been instigated by Fergus, and it didn't take me long to find that the birds had flown. I dragged our dwarfish friend into the house and left him there; then I searched the place from top to bottom. But I didn't find Anne—though it was obvious she'd been there because of the annulus."

Marks said: "But if you found the annulus, might that not mean Anne is dead? She wouldn't part with it of her own free will."

"Don't worry; she's still alive. The Sybil's Annulus heightenes one's psychic sensitivity—particularly concerning the person by whom it's been habitually worn. Anne is alive, as Donald Rathlaw and Fiona are no doubt alive. But obviously something has been planned for them, to take place with due ceremony. Witchcraft is nothing without its rituals; neither is vengeance—when planned by its practitioners."

"What do you think happened to Donald and Fiona?" asked Marks, as he hurriedly struggled into his shirt. "They wouldn't get far in their night-clothes, surely, even at that hour."

"They didn't—not walking. The reception clerk ran out after them, just in time to see them being bundled into a car, which drove quickly away—"

Marks said sharply: "He got the number?"

"No. He's had a lot of experience of honeymoon couples and it would take something very extraordinary to shake him. He concluded they'd gone off on some ribald first-night honeymoon prank with friends—"

"In nightdress and pyjamas?" snorted Marks. "The man needs his head examined!"

Kane grinned. "You'd have thought exactly the same thing, Lionel—if it had been anyone but Donald and Fiona," he said. "We all know what young people are up to these days. Nothing sacred."

"I'd like to see my Myra behaving that way!" said Marks. "I'd tan her bottom until she couldn't sit down for a week." Then he added: "You think either Fergus or Cosmo Trayle was in that car?"

"I think it was Cosmo and the Erskines. The hand-kerchief they obtained from Fiona in Aberdeen would have given Cosmo a psychic contact with her. We don't know the technique they used to establish a controlling *rapport*, but evidently they had suffi-cient confidence in it to wait for her near the hotel. She responded as expected—and Donald naturally came after her."

"So now Fergus will be coming into the picture?"

"With a prisoner of his own—Anne."

Marks nodded somberly. "There's one thing you haven't told me—how did you know I was here?"

"That was easy. I got the address of this hotel from Sir Alastair—"

"Then you've been driving all night!" Marks looked at his companion keenly. Now that daylight was flooding into the room he could see the lines of weariness on Kane's face, his dark eyes. "You must be worn out." Then a thought struck him and he added: "You drove north to Rathlaw yesterday afternoon or evening—but you could have driven up the day before. Why didn't you?"

Kane said: "I had a body to dispose of."

"The dwarf? Couldn't you have left it in the house and tipped the police off with an anonymous phone-call?"

"I could have. And the result would have been splash headlines in the press. Fergus and his pals must have left in a hurry, for they'd made no attempt to dispose of their paraphernalia. It was obvious that the place had been used for purposes of sorcery. The police would have hot-footed after the Trayles in no time at all—and you can imagine how that would help Anne. Fergus would have killed her instantly."

Marks scowled. "I didn't think of that. But of course he would have. She'd have proved too dangerous a witness! He'd have murdered her and gone safely to earth somewhere."

"Exactly. As it is, she's still alive. I thought of leaving the dwarf's body in the house, but the smell of decomposition would soon have attracted attention. So I went back again the following night, as soon as it was dark, and smuggled him out to my car."

"Where did you dump him?"

"In the River Clyde. When it's found it will be assumed he fell into the river after a fatal heart attack. Which is true."

"And yesterday?"

Ironically, Kane said: "Yesterday, after two disturbed nights and with a long night drive ahead of me, I snatched a couple of hours sleep. I also did some experiments with Anne's silver annulus. And I made a trunk call to London, to John Dyball. He should arrive in Glasgow today."

At this mention of the fourth working director of The Guardians, the Rev. John Dyball, Marks's eyes narrowed.

"You think he's going to be needed?" he asked.

Kane looked his companion directly in the face. "As I said a few minutes ago, what is planned for Donald and Fiona will take place with due ceremony. And that kind of ritual isn't performed in daylight. Do you happen to know today's date?"

"Eh?" Marks thought for a moment, his face screwed up, then said: "Why, July the thirty-first. Why? What's the point—"

"The point," Kane replied tautly, "is that tonight brings one of the four Fire Festivals of the Gaelic year. Each of them having a potent significance in witchcraft ritual. Tonight is the Eve of *Lugnasadh* or Lammas—one of the most appropriate nights for a Witches' Sabbat."

Marks went a little pale. "Then we've only a few hours to trace Anne and the others and help them get away before—"

"Precisely," said Kane. "So come on. We've wasted too much time already."

He turned and led the way out.

The two Land Rovers came to a stop at a little distance from the croft on which Lionel Marks had had his strange experience—the croft owned by Aggie Erskine.

From the two vehicles several men climbed down. Two were armed with shotguns. They were employees of the Laird of Rathlaw—Duncan and Angus. Among the party was the Laird himself. Looking desperately worried.

From the second Land Rover came Steven Kane, Lionel Marks—and Father John Dyball, Anglo-Catholic priest without a parish.

Like Marks, Dyball was in his forties, but there the resemblance ended. He was a tall, lean, ascetic man with a handsome face and an air of calm assurance about him which was seldom shattered, even in the most unnerving situations. On him Steven Kane knew that he could depend implicitly.

But not even Kane had been able to probe the mystery surrounding the cause and circumstances of Father Dyball's relinquishment of office, although there was no doubt of his fervent belief in God—and in the Devil. A well-to-do bachelor, he was no spoiled dilettante; under duress he could swear like a trooper and fight with the ferocity of a tiger.

His lack of personal ties left him free to give The Guardians, when necessary, the benefit of his knowledge and experience in the unending war against the Powers of Darkness. Only when there was doubt as to whether direct human action alone could prevail over an evil situation did Kane and the other Guardians called on Father Dyball.

It was Kane who had decided that this croft was the place where they would find Anne Ashby. He had used his pendulum and Anne's silver annulus to trace her present whereabouts by radiesthesia, and this had proved as easy as had the tracing of Fergus Trayle. Like the Hermit, Anne had very strong psychic vibrations which affected anything habitually worn or handled by her.

With a small-scale map of Scotland the experiment had given a general indication of the Rathlaw estate and the surrounding area. Then a large-scale map of that area had pin-pointed a location which Lionel Marks identified as the Erskines' farm.

"By Harry!—so that's where Anne is! And Donald and Fiona too, you can bet," Marks had exclaimed. "Just the kind of place Fergus would choose—"

" 'Men loved darkness rather than light, because their deeds were evil,' " murmured Father Dyball. "I think you're right, Steven."

Then Marks's brow had furrowed. "Isn't it more likely Fergus would have taken them to his shack at Black Loch?" he asked.

Kane had shaken his head. "It wouldn't be big enough to hold three prisoners and their guards. I'm convinced they're all at the Erskine farmhouse—tonight's Sabbat is somewhere in that area, for certain."

"In that case," Father Dyball had put in crisply, "it would be wise for us to get to the Erskine place well before nightfall."

"Of course. Once they're taken to the Sabbat we'll have a bigger crowd of degenerates to deal with."

Now Kane, his eyes narrowed, his whole body tensed for action, led the way towards the gate of the farmhouse.

There was no sight or sound of human life other than themselves when Kane quietly eased the croft gate open and went up the path to the ramshackle house.

Chapter Sixteen

Sir Alastair hurried to overtake Kane, at which point Kane stopped and beckoned to the younger of the two Castle employees.

"Duncan," he said. "You go round to the back of the farmhouse with the shotgun. Angus—" He nodded towards the other man. "You stay here with us."

"I'll go with Duncan," said Marks. He added, with a faint grin: "Just in case Jamie's water-kelpie makes an appearance. A blast from that twelve-bore would soon prove whether it was an apparition or not."

Kane and the others advanced cautiously towards the front door. The whole place seemed to be in darkness.

"I don't like it," Kane muttered. "It's too damn quiet to please me."

"The curtains are drawn, but there's no light behind them," Father Dyball pointed out. "Is it possible they've already gone?"

"We'll soon find out," said Kane grimly.

Glancing around to make sure that Father Dyball and Angus were close behind, he stepped up to the front door.

"Here goes—" he said, and knocked.

There was no reply, no sight or sound of life. Kane knocked more loudly. Then a faint movement at the window caught his eye. A woman was peering through the tattered curtains—a woman who gave him a sudden wide grin.

"Aggie's here, anyway," he said.

He banged again. The rattling of a chain on the inner side of the door followed the disappearance of the woman's face from the window. Then the door was opened a few inches. Even the sight of Angus with the shotgun did not wipe the silly smile from her face.

"Let us in, woman!" Sir Alastair ordered brusquely. This was no time for normal courtesies.

"Aye," she assented amiably. And after fumbling with the chain again, she opened the door wide and stepped aside.

Kane entered, with Father Dyball and the Laird close upon his heels. Dyball's fastidious nostrils twitched as the smell of the place assailed them.

"'I counted two and seventy stenches, all well defined, and several stinks,'" he quoted, adding: "I may have missed one or two, but I think not."

Inside the littered room was a boy they recognized instantly—Jamie, the dumb lad, who had the gift of the Horseman's Word. He was sitting on the dirt-encrusted floor, aimlessly playing with a pony's bridle. His large eyes inspected the visitors curiously, but he did not move.

"How many rooms are there?" Sir Alastair asked,

too anxious and impatient to leave the talking to Kane.

"Three," Aggie grinned. "Kitchen, bedroom and —" she made a gesture encompassing the room in which they were standing.

"We're going to search them," Sir Alastair told her.

"Aye," She remained quite unconcerned.

They soon knew why. After dragging back the curtains to let in more light, Kane searched the bedroom and Father Dyball looked into the kitchen. There was no one in either room.

The worried lines on the Laird's face deepened and he looked at Kane almost accusingly. "You said they would be here—"

Kane replied: "I said Anne Ashby was here. When I made the test in Glasgow she was. I doubt now whether your son and his wife have ever been here. But Anne has—and left only recently."

"How do you know?"

Kane lifted his right hand; in it was a length of rope, which had been knotted and then cut. He said: "I found this in the bedroom. I believe it was used to bind Anne. She must have managed to free herself and escaped through the window—the catch is broken. Aggie here knew she's gone, because an attempt has been made to re-fasten the catch on the inside."

The Laird's eyes were puzzled. "But why—"

"You mean, why hasn't she done anything about it? Like informing the Trayles—"

Sir Alastair nodded. "That's what I meant. Feeble-minded she may be, but obviously Miss Ashby had been left in her custody. Surely the first thing she would have done was warn the Trayles she'd escaped?"

155

"I think it's highly likely they're too far from the croft for either Aggie or her son to reach them. Remember, they'd have to go on foot. She probably thought the best thing to do would be to wait until somebody came to fetch Anne and break the news then."

"But what about Donald—and Fiona?" demanded Sir Alastair. "We're no nearer finding them now than we were six hours ago!"

Father Dyball leaned forward and put his hand on the Laird's shoulder. The quiet strength which flowed from him seemed to calm Sir Alastair slightly.

Dyball looked across at Kane. He said: "If Anne's on foot—and it's highly probable she is—she must be somewhere in the vicinity. I suggest you try the radiesthesia again, Steven. I think the same applies to Donald and his wife."

"I'll need something they've used," said Kane. "That means we'll have to return to the Castle."

"Then let's hurry, for God's sake!" said the Laird. He turned to Angus. "And bring those two along—" He indicated Aggie Erskine and the indifferent Jamie. "The boy is obviously in need of care—his mother isn't fit to have charge of him."

Aggie had been standing with a fixed grin on her face, showing no emotion even when they discussed her. But now her smile vanished abruptly. From her open mouth came a sudden frantic wail:

"Jamie! Ma bairn. They cannae tak' ye awa' frae yer mither—"

She made an ungainly leap and pounced on the boy. With surprising strength she plucked him up as if he were a doll.

Wriggling in her grasp he could make only an eerie hissing sound in protest.

"Put him down!" the Laird commanded sternly.

The woman glowered. "He's mine! He's ma bairn. Naebody shall tak' him. I'd rather see him—"

With fierce maternal instinct she hugged the boy to her. Then, grinning again in triumph, she put her right hand around his throat—and tightened it.

The boy choked for breath. As Kane and Father Dyball rushed at her to release him, she beat furiously at them with her free arm. Her son was dangling from her throttling grip.

The boy's face was already cyanosed.

Reluctant to actually strike her and knock her unconscious, Kane secured a grip on her throat. But before her murderous fingers began to loosen the boy's bulging eyes were glassy. When he dropped to the floor he landed in a slack heap.

Angus, peering pale-faced over Father Dyball's shoulder, gasped: "The crazy boggart's kilt him—"

Father John Dyball dropped quickly to one knee to feel the boy's pulse. "It's stopped," he said.

He leaned across the boy, who was no longer breathing, and began to administer the kiss of life. He glanced up at Kane.

"You others go ahead. I'll do what I can here—"

Kane said: "It's imperative we all leave at once—and together. We'll have to take the boy with us. I'll help you, John."

Father Dyball lifted the boy and went out of the house at a run. Aggie Erskine trotted behind, with Angus's shotgun prodding her back. Satisfied in her dim mind that no one would now be able to take the boy from her, she went without protest.

Lionel Marks and Duncan joined the party as they reached the two Land Rovers. At a word from Kane they took their seats in the back of one of the vehicles and guarded the woman. Marks, eyeing her warily, felt his own hand go instinctively to his throat, remembering the last time he had met Aggie and the feel of her iron hands upon him.

Kane lifted Jamie into the back of the other Land Rover, where Father Dyball began immediately to resume his attempts at resuscitation. Angus took the wheel of the Land Rover which held Aggie Erskine, Duncan and Marks, with the Laird seated beside him. But before going back to his own vehicle Kane said quickly to Father Dyball:

"I'll keep my eyes open for Anne. Good luck with the boy—"

John Dyball was too absorbed in his desperate task to answer. A moment later Kane was driving off, heading at top speed towards the Castle.

Already the sun was half-obscured by a range of low-lying distant hills, and a chill shadow was spreading across the land.

Ten minutes later Kane gave a sudden exclamation:

"Anne!"

He sent the Land Rover swerving towards a distant trudging figure, half-swallowed in the gloom. The figure turned at the sound of the heavy vehicle.

Anne Ashby it proved to be. She was trudging along tiredly. Recognizing Kane's voice, she hurried back to him.

"Thank God!" she said as he came to a stop beside her. "I've been going round in circles. This damn country—"

He gave her a quick, searching glance to reassure himself that she had come to no bodily harm. He said: "Get in. We've just come from the Erskine place—"

"You've been there?" Annie's voice was startled as she scrambled up into the front seat next to him.

"I knew you were there. We hoped to find Donald Rathlaw and Fiona there, too. The Trayles kidnapped them on their wedding night. I used your annulus to trace you to the farmhouse, then I found the ropes and guessed you'd escaped."

The second Rover drew up beside them. From the back floated a crazy crooning, previously inaudible, an eerie rendering of an old Highland lullaby.

Anne recognized the voice. "You've got Aggie and the boy!"

Before Kane could reply Father John Dyball climbed slowly down from the back of the Land Rover and came towards them. His eyes burned tiredly in his ravaged face and his breathing was uneven.

"The boy's dead," he said quietly. "I did what I could, but there was no hope."

Anne's dark eyes clouded. The ending of a young life, whether afflicted or not, is always tragic.

"Poor Jamie," she said. "How did it happen?"

"His mother strangled him," said Kane, brutally.

"Strangled him? But she doted on—"

"She did it to stop us taking him away from her. But I'm afraid we can't waste time grieving over Jamie. We've got to find Donald and Fiona. There'll be a Sabbat tonight if my guess is right."

"Yes. And I was to be the altar," said Anne.

"Do you know where it was to be held?"

"No. But the Trayles were going to send someone back to the croft to take me there."

Kane's eyes gleamed. "That's what I thought!

159

There's a quicker way of finding young Donald and his wife now than by radiesthesia."

He jumped down from the Land Rover. From the other vehicle Lionel Marks and the Laird were approaching.

Anxious, impatient words erupted from Sir Alastair.

"For God's sake, Mr. Kane, let's get back to the Castle! Can't you see—it'll be dark in half an hour! If we don't find Donald—" He raised shaking hands. "I should have notified the police. They would have been searching for him by this time with helicopters—"

"That action would have signed his immediate death warrant," said Kane curtly. "The reason your son is still alive is because the police are *not* hunting for him—and for the Trayles." He grasped the Laird by the shoulders. "I appreciate your anxiety, Sir Alastair, but now we have a more concrete hope—a more direct way of discovering where your son has been taken. I want you to send your two men back to the Castle with the Erskine woman and the boy—"

Marks broke in. "How is he?" He looked at Father Dyball, and the priest slowly shook his head. He had already taken off his coat and was placing it over the small body in the rear of the Land Rover. As he did so he murmured a quiet prayer.

Marks winced, feeling a sour taste surge up from his stomach into his throat. For a moment he thought he would be sick, and had to fight for control. No matter what Jamie had done, or whose evil instrument he had been, he was only a child and Marks had a soft spot for all children.

Kane went on: "You go with Duncan and Angus

160

back to the Castle, Sir Alastair. Take one of the shotguns; you may need it. The rest of us will return to the farmhouse."

The Laird said, in a hollow voice: "My men can go, but I am coming with you, Mr. Kane. If there is any hope of finding my son, I want to be there!"

Kane nodded. There was no time for argument. "Very well," he said. "But tell your men to get going now." He looked at Father Dyball. The priest lifted Jamie's body and carried it slowly across to the other Land Rover, where he placed the boy at Aggie's feet. The sight of her lifeless son had a tranquilizing effect on the crooning woman, assuring her that he was safe from those who would have taken him.

Kane watched the truck head towards the Castle, then turned his own Land Rover around in the direction of the croft. Anne and Father Dyball were in the back with Sir Alastair and Lionel Marks was beside Kane, with a shotgun across his knees.

The one-time agent was strangely quiet, for Jamie's death had affected him more than he cared to admit. But he made an effort to shake off his depression when Kane nudged him, not too gently.

"This is no time for brooding, Lionel. There's grim work ahead of us tonight. You've seen more of the farm than we have—is there anywhere we can hide?"

Marks thought. "I didn't see any outhouses at all—but I noticed an old tarpaulin we could throw over the Land Rover. If we park it under the trees ten-to-one it won't be spotted."

Despite the darkness now shrouding the countryside, Kane had not switched on the Land Rover's lights. He became aware of the Laird's head craning forward from under the hood of the truck; Sir Alastair had been listening, avid for a shred of hope.

Kane, sensing his anxiety, said: "This way should be quicker, Sir Alastair—quicker than going all the way back to the Castle to hunt for them with the pendulum. When the men come to the farm for Anne, they can take *us* to the Sabbat as well."

"But how do you know they will come?" asked the Laird. "We've no proof—"

"They'll come," said Kane. "You should know Fergus Trayle by this time, Sir Alastair. Do you think he'll forego the degrading ordeal he has planned for Anne? He proposes to use her as a human altar for his vile rituals, then as a victim of the orgy to follow."

A shudder ran down the Laird's rugged frame. "All this is out of my province, Mr. Kane. I must trust you to deal with it—and God help my son and Fiona."

No lights showed at the windows of the farmhouse when Kane braked at the gate. A reconnaissance on foot confirmed that the place was deserted.

During the next five minutes Kane and Marks worked to restore a sense of normalcy to the ramshackle house. They drew the curtains and shut the door. Then Kane drove the Land Rover to the rear, parking it close to to the wall so that when it was covered with the tarpaulin it would, except under careful scrutiny, look like part of the building.

Then he and Marks climbed back into the front seats, lowered the tarpaulin over the windscreen and radiator, and all five settled down.

The waiting time was surprisingly short.

Chapter Seventeen

For a while the only sound inside the Land Rover was the sound of breathing, and restless, impatient movements from Sir Alastair. Then, into the external stillness, came the purr of a distant motor. Gradually the purr grew louder, nearer.

Within minutes it was near enough for them to estimate that it was approaching the front gateway of the farm. And then, abruptly, the sound was cut off altogether.

There was a murmur of distant masculine voices, then a crunch of feet along the path leading to the front door of the farmhouse. That sound too, grew louder, nearer.

Kane felt a movement beside him as Lionel Marks took a firmer grip on the shotgun.

Now came a knocking on the door. A peremptory knocking. A pause, and more knocking. Then a longer pause—no doubt while the door was being tried—followed by a further tramp of feet, this time inside the house.

Even from where the Guardians and the Laird waited, they could clearly hear hoarse exclamations of surprise. Evidently the one thing the visitors had not expected had been to find the house deserted.

Kane said very quietly to Marks: "Now!"

Turning towards the hood of the Land Rover, he whispered to the others: "You three take up positions against the rear windows. If you can smash them at a psychological moment, it should have considerable effect. Make them wonder just how large our forces are. Right!"

" 'Let your loins be girded about, and your lights burning'," murmured Father Dyball.

He had a fund of such sayings, which he would drop in at various appropriate—and inappropriate—moments. Kane never quite knew whether he was serious or not; at times he had a feeling that the Rev. John Dyball spoke tongue-in-cheek. But his conversational manner did not detract from his prowess as a fighting man when the moment for action arrived.

Pushing the edge of the tarpaulin aside, Kane jumped out. Marks joined him with the shotgun, at the front of the house. Sir Alastair, Father Dyball and Anne took up their stances at the rear.

The house's interior was dimly lit by an oil lamp. The parking lights of a stationary vehicle, similar to a Land Rover but with a silhouette which told Kane it was an Austin Gypsy, showed at the farm gateway.

Kane and Marks simultaneously sprinted past the front window to the open doorway, from which light fanned out reluctantly over the path.

There Marks lifted the shotgun and levelled it. Kane rapped out:

"Keep quite still, my friend!"

The man standing in the living room instantly froze.

There was a loud crash of splintering glass at the house—Father John and his companions obeying instructions—and immediately afterwards another man came running from the bedroom into the living-room. He came to an abrupt and startled halt at sight of Kane and Marks.

"What the hell—" he began.

Kane and Marks stepped into the room. Marks grinned into the astonished faces of the two men and said, ironically:

"Sorry, boys, but Annie doesn't live here any more . . ."

There was a scrambling sound in the bedroom, explained when Anne emerged from it, having climbed through the broken window. Father Dyball was close on her heels and a moment later the Laird—less agile—came hurrying through the front door.

"Only two of them?" he asked. "Is there anyone in their car?"

Kane looked at Anne. "Just check, will you—from a safe distance, of course."

The two men, frozen beneath the menace of the shotgun, were just beginning to thaw when Anne returned, to report that the Austin Gypsy was un-occupied and unattended.

"So this is the full bag!" Marks commented, with satisfaction. "All we need now are the rest of the black sheep."

Kane said urbanely, "Well, we only need one of these two. We can eliminate the other. Which of you wants to be the survivor?"

Both men were now facing him. One of them looked distinctly apprehensive at Kane's words, but the other, who had seen Father Dyball come into the room, jeered disbelievingly:

"Huh! A priest—connive at murder! Tell us an-other."

" 'Judge not according to the appearance,' " said Dyball. "There are other lives at stake—far more important than yours." He continued, unctuously: "Execution of the body is sometimes justifiable as the only way to save the soul. Which of you prefers to save his body and ease his guilty soul by guiding us to the Sabbat?"

"—on the understanding," Kane warned, "that if he misleads us, his own end will be very prompt."

"And very unpleasant," added Marks, moving the shotgun slightly. "I shall aim for the head. Thus your relatives will be spared a last sight of your ugly faces."

The atmosphere of the room was now charged with tension. The two men had begun to realize that these people who spoke so lightly of 'execution' did so because they were accustomed to dealing with the darkest deeds of mankind.

Anne Ashby said: "Let me eliminate the one we don't need. After all, the reason for their coming here was to eliminate *me*."

That request, coming so calmly and with such horrifying indifference from the tall, beautiful woman confronting them, completed the demoralization of the two men. One of the disadvantages of being ruthless themselves was that it made it easy for them to believe in the ruthlessness of others. No doubt they had faith in the Trayles' ability to avenge them, but they did not want to be avenged posthumously.

Neither would admit to being afraid for his own skin, but now both volunteered without further hesitation to take their captors to the Sabbat.

The man who had scoffed at the threat of 'elimination' gave a sneering reason for his readiness to co-operate.

166

"I'll take you there," he grinned. "Why not? The Hermit will be pleased to see you coming like lambs to the slaughter." He pointed at the shotgun in Marks's hands. "D'you imagine that thing will be of any use against the Hermit's powers? Sure, I'll take you!"

"So will I," said his companion instantly. "Like he says, what can you do against—"

"Your loud-mouthed friend will be quite sufficient," Kane cut in. "Lionel—dispose of the redundant one, will you?"

Grasping his chosen guide by the collar, Kane swung him around and marched him out of the house. He went quickly to the rear, closely followed by the Laird and Anne. They dragged the tarpaulin off the truck. The Laird was climbing into the back when the night stillness was shattered by the blast of a shotgun.

Even in the gloom Kane could see that his captive's face had gone deathly white. "So you did mean murder!" he blurted hoarsely. "With a priest, too . . ."

Kane did not think it necessary to explain that undoubtedly Marks had driven his prisoner into a safe corner, then fired the shotgun out through the open doorway. The effect on the survivor was very satisfactory.

With the Laird and Anne in the back, and the now voiceless guide seated beside him, Kane drove the Land Rover round to the front of the farmhouse. Marks and Father Dyball came out and shut the door behind them. Inside was an ominous silence.

"Finished?" asked Kane with what his unhappy passenger considered a quite unjustifiable indifference.

" 'We have done that which was our duty to do,' " said Father Dyball, his face expressionless.

"And you call yourself a priest!" the man snarled. "Why, you're nothing but bloody murderers, the pair of you!"

"Shut up!" said Kane. Father Dyball and Marks climbed into the vehicle. Kane accelerated, then stopped.

"Just a minute," he said. "Keep an eye on this beggar while I put that Gypsy out of action—just in case any more of his pals show up."

Within a minute he had removed the rotor-arm and rendered the vehicle unusable. When the man in the house finally escaped from the ropes Marks and Father Dyball had knotted around him, he would have no chance of overtaking them or of warning the Trayles that they were on their way to the Sabbat.

Accelerating again, Kane snapped at the man beside him: "Now—start directing us. We've no time to waste but if you try to double-cross us, it'll be the worse for you."

"I've re-loaded the shot-gun," said Marks. He added, apologetically: "I'm afraid I wasn't very accurate just now—I only blew half his head off. But he's dead now, anyway."

"You devils!" ground out the man. Then he felt the barrel of the shot-gun touch lightly against the back of his neck, and he began to talk . . .

Swiftly then, Kane piloted the Land Rover in the direction their sullen guide outlined.

Mr. Rodney Pritchard was surprisingly young to have achieved success and wealth as a City of London property speculator. That he had done so attested

168

not to hard work and honest endeavor, but to shady dealing and chicanery.

Rodney was completely without scruples. He would take the widow's mite with as little compunction as the millionaire's check, and during the transaction, would manage to divert a large proportion of both into his own pocket by giving far less than value for money.

By the time he was thirty he had as much as he could possibly need—and he was a greedy man. Wise investment had secured him a fortune and the main thing now was to enjoy it. This he succeeded in doing very well indeed, until by the time he was thirty-five he had sampled every conceivable kind of flesh-pot.

One thing led to another and what there was to learn of debauchery, depravity and vice Rodney Pritchard learned quickly. From the proceeds of his ill-gotten gains he had bought himself a large house, complete with shooting lodge, in the Scottish Highlands, where he threw innumerable parties. Perhaps orgies would have been a better word.

But after a while he began to realize that he was bored. He wanted new experiences, new titillations for his jaded palate. And he found them when chance, by way of a business deal, crossed his path with that of Cosmo Trayle.

Like recognized like. Entry into Cosmo's circle was not difficult; the rest came with surprising ease. From a mere initiate Rodney Pritchard progressed to full-fledged member, then to more than a member. He became not only the Trayles' closest associate, but their helper and confidante.

While outwardly preserving the appearance and habits of a prominent business man, he secretly indulged in the vilest rituals attendant upon occultism and the Left Hand Path. Unlike Fergus and Cosmo Trayle, however, he had no hypnotic or Satanic powers—and was probably all the more evil because of that fact. A frustrated man is often a vicious man; and Rodney's sense of failure in one direction caused him to emphasize his peculiar abilities in others.

Now, looking a little out of place in his expensive suit of Harris tweed, he stood in the lounge of his Highland shooting lodge facing the two Trayle brothers, Fergus and Cosmo.

Cosmo too was wearing a tweed country suit, but Fergus had resumed the cassock-like garment that was his usual outer garb.

Rodney was excited. Tonight the Trayles had promised to initiate him into the blackest of all the Satanic rites and he was looking forward to it in the same way that a child looks forward to its first birthday party. This night was to witness the ultimate in horror and devilry and when it was over Cosmo had promised him that—as a true emissary of the Devil—he would become possessed of the same magical powers as both himself and Fergus.

That their evil machinations entailed the death of young Donald Rathlaw, and possibly others, did not worry Rodney Pritchard one jot. Even the fact that the Laird was a more or less close neighbor made no difference. He would quite cheerfully have sacrificed members of his own family if by so doing he could gain his heart's desire. If he could become, truly, a Satanist of unlimited powers.

Pritchard said, frowning slightly: "There's only one thing worries me, Cosmo. Young Donald's death must be made to look like an accident. I don't want any police investigations."

"You needn't be afraid of that," Cosmo replied.

"Donald's corpse will be found a long way from here—somewhere near Dunoon."

"And what about the girl—his wife?"

"It's all planned. When young Rathlaw's body is found the police won't look any further than his bride. As a matter of fact, our fair Fiona is going to kill her husband—*and* confess to the police."

An expression of uneasiness crossed Pritchard's face. He looked skeptical.

"She wouldn't kill her own husband. I know your powers, Cosmo, but not even you two could make her do that." Then his eyes narrowed. "I suppose you think you can make her do it under hypnosis? I'm no authority, but I understand that even hypnotism can't make people do anything they have strong moral objections to doing."

Cosmo smiled again. "You're quite right about that, though our influence over people is not limited to the hypnotic, as you well know by now. But overcoming the difficulty you mention will make no great demands on our powers. At the Sabbat you will see how it is done."

Fergus gave a coarse laugh. "And the full proceedings will provide something just as interesting. I'm sending a couple of men to bring back that female spy I caught in Glasgow. After young Rathlaw has been disposed of, she will supply the altar for some fascinating rituals."

Pritchard nodded eagerly. "The glen in the woods? And afterwards . . . you promised—"

"Tonight," Fergus prophesied, turning to gaze out of the lounge window, "you'll see such things as you never believed possible. Things you thought were just mediaeval fantasies and ignorant superstitions."

171

He seemed to forget the presence of his host and went on talking, in a murmuring reverie.

"Tonight is the Eve of *Lugnasadh*. There's magic in the mountains and the spirits of the glen are stirring. There'll be oak-leaves for the believers and the warlock's hazel of all wisdom for the Hermit of Black Loch. Here in the Highlands, where witchcraft was nurtured and where I have brooded in the seclusion and the darkness . . . have communed with the Unseen, till I am now at the peak of my powers—"

"Powers which you will help *me* to attain?" Rodney Pritchard put in, and there were beads of sweat on his face. "That was your promise for allowing the Sabbat to be held here, on my land—"

Fergus went on as though he had not spoken.

"But one thing eludes me . . . Why? The achievement that eludes all the prophets, the power to foresee one's own future. Why is that veiled from me? From Cosmo too? Or is it veiled? It cannot be that we have no future . . .

"Young Donald Rathlaw has no future, that I have sworn and that I now prophesy. But what—who—is obscuring the dawn after this night's Sabbat? Why do I know that things of terror and mystery will come to pass this Lammas Eve, yet even I know not what lies beyond the veil of Lammas dawn . . ."

He turned back to survey the room and under his magnetic, malevolent eyes, Rodney Pritchard felt suddenly afraid.

In that yellowish, lambent stare was the dreadful rousing of some nocturnal creature ready to set out on a mission too terrible for daylight and too abominable to be named.

For a moment even Pritchard, ready to connive

at murder for his own evil purposes, quailed inwardly in the presence of an evil greater than any he could ever have visualized. Of wickedness needing no motivation other than the fulfilment of its own depraved nature.

In that awesome moment he felt the vertigo of a man who has looked down into the abyss of Hell.

Chapter Eighteen

In the darkness of a shallow glen near the center of Rodney Pritchard's extensive shoot, a blazing bonfire cast a lurid, flickering glow on the intent faces of the concourse of people surrounding it. From all directions rose a mass murmur of expectancy.

From somewhere on the outskirts of the throng came a faint whisper of pipe music, rising and falling in a haunting coronach of aching desolation, bittersweet with the mournful spirit of deserted lochs and mist-shrouded hills.

All eyes were concentrated on a tall figure seated in a high-backed Jacobean armchair set on a mound which commanded a view of the congregation.

A human figure . . . from the neck downwards. Clad in a purple, cassock-like garment familiar to most of the depraved throng. But above the shoulders —un-human.

173

The great head was the furry, horned head of an animal.

At a distance of a half-dozen yards from either side of the enthroned figure a flaring torch was spiked to the ground, each with an attendant acolyte standing by. From censers placed at intervals around the fire wafted the odor of hemp, its acrid fumes polluting the night air.

The grotesque hybrid creature in the chair was sitting motionless. Beside it stood a man in a similar cassock but with his human face unconcealed. The man called Cosmo Trayle.

The soft, somber wailing of the pipes gave way to a martial theme, reinforced with the beat of a drum. The atmosphere became tense, brittle with a tingling anticipation.

As the rhythm and pitch of the music mounted to a blood-stirring crescendo, into the circle of red light cast by the fire came two men. They were carrying an inert human figure—that of a girl.

Her hair needed no tinting by the fire-glow. It was red in actuality. She was wearing only a diaphanous garment that would have been appropriate as a bridal nightdress. Its thin material clung to the contours of her body. Lascivious eyes now concentrated on her and the expectant murmur became one of imminent gratification.

Unconscious, the red-haired girl was flung down on the turf at the feet of the fantastic, seated hybrid. The drum-beat increased in volume and tempo until it was a mass intoxicant.

Hoarse voices began a senseless chant in rhythm with the drum. The unconscious girl stirred.

The chanting became louder, faster. Again the girl stirred. And as the chanting and the drumming beat at her senses with frenzied insistence, her eyes opened.

They moved dazedly in their sockets as her dulled brain tried to assemble and interpret the chaotic impressions received by eyes and ears.

At last, with a great effort, she raised herself to one elbow, staring about her like someone in a waking nightmare.

And then her wondering, shrinking gaze rose—and met the glassy stare of the Goat.

Instinctively Fiona Rathlaw cringed.

Even the workings of her own mind seemed remote from her. But into and through that mental haziness the fearsome, grotesque animal head on the seated body loomed as the most sharply-focused and comprehensible object in a reeling world.

Mentally magnified, it filled her field of view. She cowered away from it with a low and husky babble of delirium pouring from her mouth.

Then, like a telephoto picture zooming away into a longshot, it receded, to allow her to see the whole figure again—and the figure of a man standing beside the chair.

She saw the man's lips move. Distorted by the pounding in her ears, words came to her. Floated to her as through the woolly veil of high fever.

"We understand your distress . . . It is natural for a woman to be distressed when she has been newly widowed . . ."

Widowed!

Even in Fiona's delirium that word clawed at her mind.

It could not be true. Someone was teasing her—cruelly, obscenely. She began to whimper and her thinly-covered breasts shook under the diaphanous garment.

Teasing her . . . It wasn't right; it wasn't fair, when all she wanted to do was to relax into this warm, billowing cloud of cotton-wool waiting to receive her weary body and drowsy mind. If only those drum-beats would stop . . .

The voice of the man in the cassock came again. He was smiling at her, and there was a note of sympathy in his voice which, even in her bemused state, Fiona sensed was spurious.

"It is distressing for any young girl to be widowed . . . but for a bride—and a bride in name only . . ."

The drum-beat pounding into her reeling brain roused an aggressive instinct.

"I am not a widow!" she cried, trying to make herself heard above that maddening din.

"Indeed you are," the voice went on. "And not even by natural causes. Your bridegroom had an enemy. An enemy who killed him with—this!"

Now something jutted from the speaker's right hand. Something that glinted red and deadly in the firelight. A knife.

His smile widening, the standing man in the cassock tossed the knife down to her. It dropped soundlessly on the turf.

She did not look at it. Instead she pushed herself up off the ground and into a kneeling position, staring up painfully at her informant.

"Not Donald . . ." she murmured thickly. "He isn't dead . . ."

"I'm afraid he is, my dear. Killed with that knife, by his enemy . . ."

She glanced down and picked up the knife. If it had stabbed a man, it had since been cleaned . . .

Why wouldn't that maddening drumming, that terrible chanting, stop?

"What enemy?" she demanded, with a childish grimace of disbelief. "Donald has no enemies . . ."

Raising his eyebrows mockingly the standing man pointed a finger at the seated beast in the chair.

Adrenalin pumped into Fiona's bloodstream, flooding her muscles with a surge of fantastic energy. So that was why she had found that hideous creature so hateful? He had killed Donald . . .

With a screech of hatred and fury, Fiona scooped up the knife, leaped to her feet and hurled herself at the motionless monster in the imitation throne.

With blazing eyes, she thrust the knife deep into the robed chest beneath the head of the glassy-eyed Goat.

The hideous head toppled and slumped over on to one shoulder.

The drumming and the chanting had stopped. In the sudden silence she let her arm fall, drained of energy as suddenly as she had been infused with it. The knife dropped from her limp fingers.

The man who had jeered at her was now grinning fiendishly. Still dazed, Fiona watched him reach across to the seated Goat and wrench. The animal head, an immense artificial one, came away between his hands.

Fiona stared—and stared.

The head that was now slumped over on to one shoulder was the head of a man—a young man with a gag tied around his mouth. His eyes were closed, his face drained of all color, in horrifying contrast to the spreading stain on the front of the robe he wore.

But the leaping bonfire flames illuminated him

plainly enough. Fiona shrieked. Shriek after shriek tore through the night as she recognized her victim. Donald, her husband.

Her cries were drowned before the shock-waves of mocking laughter that suddenly beat upon her from all sides. Her mind and senses cowered and cringed from the derision of those voices, the implication of the whole terrifying scene.

Words floated into her swimming consciousness from the man still standing beside that ominously drooping figure in the throne.

"You killed him . . . you killed him. You killed your bridegroom. He is dead and *you* killed him."

Fiona clapped her hands over her ears to shut out the echoing, hideous accusation. She could still hear it. She could still see that limp body, with the ever-spreading scarlet stain on its chest.

She closed her eyes. But in the darkness she herself created she gave little shuddering whimpers which shook her whole body.

"Donald . . . Donald . . ." she moaned. "I didn't mean to do it. I didn't mean to do it. Donald . . ."

The babble quickened to an incoherent slither of sounds—before her mind dissolved and she collapsed unconscious across the blood-stained knife.

When the Land Rover crossed the boundary of the Pritchard property, Sir Alastair Rathlaw was craned over Steven Kane's shoulder and muttering an agitation.

"Hurry, hurry . . ." He suddenly started in surprise. "But we're on Pritchard's land!" he ejaculated.

"Pritchard?"

"Deals in property. He bought the place a few

178

months ago. But surely *he* can't be in league with the Trayles—"

"Anything is possible," said Kane briefly. "And from the look of that glow ahead I'd say the Sabbat is being held there."

He jammed his elbow into the prisoner. "Is that where they're holding the Sabbat?" he demanded.

The man did not answer. Then, on the other side, he felt the muzzle of the shotgun push against his ribs.

"Yes," he muttered sullenly.

"In that case," said Kane, "we can dispense with you."

He stopped the truck and jumped out. Reaching up, he dragged the man out by the scruff of his neck and hurled him forcibly to the ground.

"You'll never get there in time!" the man sneered. "It's more than a mile away—"

"We'll make it," said Kane.

He jumped back into the Land Rover, leaving the man standing uncertainly in the middle of the desolate heathland. However fast he might run he would not be able to reach that glowing bonfire before they did.

"Hurry, hurry!" pleaded the Laird again.

In the darkness, and with only sidelights on, Kane drove as fast as he dared over the rough country towards that distant glow. A glow which became larger and more lurid every minute.

It soon became obvious that glow visible from the Land Rover came from above bonfire, that the fire itself was hidden in some deep depression. So when the ground began to slope downwards, Kane switched off his sidelights.

Less than a minute later the bonfire itself could be seen, partly screened by trees and with the dark silhouettes of people moving across it. It was at the bottom of a shallow glen.

Suddenly Father John Dyball leaned forward and put his hand upon Kane's knee. "Out of the car, quickly!" he said. There was an urgency in his voice which none of them had heard before.

They tumbled out in a heap—Kane, Sir Alastair, Marks, still carrying the shotgun, and Anne Ashby. And as with one accord their eyes went from the flickering light of the bonfire toward Father Dyball a hush descended on them.

John Dyball stood staring up at the darkened sky. They could see that his face was paper-white. Beads of perspiration ran down his face. But his eyes burned with a terrible, intense fire and his whole body held the rigidity of someone turned to stone.

Then he moved. His hand went up to his throat in a violent gesture and from around it he tore the golden crucifix he always wore. It came away with the broken links of the chain still dangling and the priest raised it to the full length of his arm, pushing it upwards as though he would push it into the sky.

From his lips exploded words in Latin. Kane thought the speaker was in the grip of some kind of seizure. Then he realized that Father Dyball was praying, invoking God's help with all the strength and power at his command because he knew that in that moment something so dreadful was happening down among the trees that no human aid could reach it in time.

The others felt as though they were watching the figure of some great Avenger; it seemed as though muted thunder rolled from between his lips and the golden crucifix in his up-reaching hand flashed forth in lightning. They stood, awed into immobility, as though, like Dyball himself, they too had been turned to stone.

Then Father Dyball relaxed. He stopped speaking and his arm fell limply to his side as though all the strength had gone from it. Quickly, he recovered. He thrust the gleaming crucifix into his pocket and turned his pale face towards his companions.

"Now!" he cried.

All began to run down the ragged slope. The intervening trees revealed the weirdly dancing figures at the bottom of the glen only intermittently, but they were in time to see Fiona as she fell, the bloodstained knife still in her grasp.

The mob noises were now rising to a baying crescendo.

Steven Kane and the Laird were in the lead as they stumbled and ran down the long, steep slope, dodging between the trees and bushes. The glen was already growing darker; the fire was dying down.

The Satanists were making so much noise that they obviously heard nothing of Kane and his companions. But Kane could now see what lay on the opposite side of the diminishing flames, aided by the additional light from the two spiked torches. He saw the two male acolytes and the big black cabinet, in it the seated figure of a bearded man wearing a dark cassock.

"Fergus Trayle!" panted Marks.

But Sir Alastair's attention was not on the man in the cabinet. As though petrified, he was staring at another cassocked figure—that of the young man on the throne.

The Laird gave a cry of unbearable anguish and staggered as though a bullet had found his heart.

"It's Donald!" he shouted. "My son! And those fiends have killed him—"

Kane made a grab at him, but he was too late. An instant later the Laird had reached the foot of the slope and was racing like a madman across the clearing, straight towards his motionless son.

Chapter Nineteen

Steven Kane, Father Dyball and Marks reached the bonfire less than a dozen yards behind Sir Alastair. As they approached the gleeful shouts turned to cries of alarm; some of the figures turned and began to run with astonishing speed up the other side of the slope and into the trees.

But Cosmo and Fergus Trayle stood their ground. Behind them stood Rodney Pritchard, his face ashen, sheer terror rooting him to the spot. Exposure, prison, ruin . . . these thoughts ran across his mind like frightened rabbits across a field.

Marks was still holding the shotgun. Now he lifted and pointed it at the figure of Cosmo Trayle. A silence descended upon the clearing.

"All right, Trayle," said Kane, clearly and loudly. "The game's up—"

Cosmo continued to stare fixedly at Marks. "You pathetic fool," he said. "Do you really think you can use that thing on me? Try! Try to fire it—"

Nothing loath, Marks pressed the trigger. Or tried to. But his fingers would not move; they felt stiff and curiously numbed. Sweating, he exerted all his will-power, but he had no more control over his trigger-finger than over a muscle in cramp. His fingers remained rigid.

Kane groaned, sensing what had happened. Cosmo Trayle's *rapport* with Marks had not been entirely eradicated by Kane's subsequent hypnosis. Enough of that subconscious influence lingered for him to be able to reassert an instant control over his one-time victim.

"Quickly!" snapped Kane. "Give me the gun!"

"Throw it!" snarled Cosmo.

Marks lifted his arm and threw the gun with all his strength towards the bonfire. It fell short but miraculously, did not go off. Before either Kane or Father Dyball could move, Cosmo suddenly lifted his arms and addressed the clearing.

"Don't be afraid, my friends. These fools cannot harm us. I will prove this to you—and when I have done so, we will destroy them as we are empowered to destroy all who attempt to come between us and the Great Master. Watch . . ."

He pointed a stubby finger towards Fergus, still sitting rigidly in the black cabinet. The bearded Hermit had not moved during all the time Kane and his companions had been in the glen, and he seemed relaxed as though asleep. Suddenly, with his eyes still closed, he raised his arms.

From the wide sleeves of his cassock his hands

protruded. Slowly the fingers splayed—and from their tips came tiny weird flashes of blue light that grew and extended like miniature lightning.

Kane had seen such sparkling from the tips of ships' masts in thunderstorms—the electrical discharge known as St. Elmo's Fire.

Now Kane stood quite still, only vaguely aware of the Laird's figure stooped over his son, and of Fiona, semi-conscious and still whimpering a few yards away. He realized that the battle had moved from the physical to the psychical plane.

Cosmo's voice came again. "We are here to pursue our quest for the esoteric knowledge that is Power. My brother is now in trance—he will lift for us the Veil of the Unseen . . ."

The St. Elmo's Fire was still giving an uncanny blue radiance to the Hermit's satyr-like face. Cosmo stopped it with a sudden swift gesture. The fire died away from the Hermit's fingers and his hands dropped.

"Watch!" commanded Cosmo, and his voice rang eerily across the glen, holding all spellbound. "You are about to see things which will convince you once and for all that nothing can stand against us! Our power is drawn from Darkness. Only fools believe that truth is beauty and that ultimate power is benevolent. Tonight my brother is going to bring you physical materializations of our historical predecessors, initiates who found in the Highlands the Dark Power we have sought. Which we now command!"

Once more he raised his hands to silence an excited murmur. As if against their will Kane and his companions stood listening.

Fergus Trayle was still inert. From his mouth and nostrils something faint and nebulous was beginning to stream. In the fire-glow it looked vaporously pink, but it must have been white or grey.

It was exuding steadily from the Hermit's facial orifices—a luminous cloud which gradually began to form into irregular shapes.

And on the night air was an odor like that of ozone mingled with the sickly-sweet smell of death.

Kane knew what it was. *Ectoplasm*.

Ectoplasm . . . the stuff of materialized phantoms.

An ideoplastic substance which could be sculpted into recognizable forms by the subconscious mind of the medium, or could be the material form manifested by a discarnate intelligence.

Now Kane understood why the bonfire had been allowed to die down and why the two flaming torches had been extinguished.

Ectoplasm was extremely sensitive to light. If suddenly so exposed, it would instanteously snap back, like elastic, into the body of the medium, inflicting hemorrhage and even death.

Most materialization mediums could operate only in complete darkness. Only a few could tolerate any light at all, and this had to be only a dim red glow. Fergus Trayle was evidently among the most exceptionally powerful.

Kane saw eyes forming in the nebulous, luminous mass. Then the surrounding ectoplasm molded itself into the features of the face of a beautiful woman.

"Isabel Goudie, most famous witch of the North of Scotland . . ."

Cosmo Trayle's voice, flat, carefully modulated, might have been that of a courier on a Continental coach-tour.

The mass of ectoplasm spread, appearing to solidify, producing another pair of eyes in another human face. The haughty face of a bearded man.

"Sir Robert Gordon, wizard of Gordonstoun. . ."

More and more ectoplasm was exuding from the Hermit, and as it did so his huge body seemed to shrink.

The next of the phantom faces began to lose its definition. Then in its place appeared a new face. A man's.

"Doctor John Fian, the Edinburgh sorcerer . . ."

By now this face too had lost its distinct features, to be replaced by those of a woman.

"Agnes Sampson, a witch of Doctor Fian's coven . . ."

Every man and woman in the clearing, Kane and his companions included, stood turned towards the Hermit, watching in mingled fascination, horror and dismay.

Nobody moved or spoke, as if held in some evil spell.

"Geillie Duncan, another witch . . ."

And then somebody did move. It was Father John Dyball. He stepped forward, his tall lean figure moving with a slow and even pace. He thrust his hand into his pocket and from it withdrew the golden crucifix, with its length of broken chain.

He lifted it. He began to pray, again in Latin, his deep, sombre voice rising above the higher notes of Cosmo Trayle. Again the words seemed to roll across the glen like muted thunder.

"I exorcise thee, thou creatures of Hell, in the

name of the Holy, Blessed and Glorious Trinity . . . the Alpha and Omega . . ."

The ectoplasm was still forming, new faces beginning to appear. The Hermit's body seemed all at once to become even more shrunken. Cosmo's own voice faltered, then rose higher.

". . . the servants of our Great Master . . ."

In his right hand Father Dyball gripped the cross. He raised it, thrusting it out before him towards Fergus Trayle.

"In the name of the Father, the Son, and the Holy Ghost . . ."

A spear of dazzling light shot suddenly from the center of the crucifix. It could have been a reflection from the leaping tongues of flame, magnified and directed purely by chance. But Kane knew that it was not.

As though the clouds had parted and sent down a shaft of lightning, the ray blazed a path across the clearing. It touched the spreading, wreathing ectoplasm—and the whole palpitating mass instantaneously vanished.

Simultaneously, from the bearded Hermit in the black cabinet ripped a shriek of mortal agony. A sheet of flame seemed to envelop him, behind which could be seen his writhing figure; there was a stench of burning and corruption and as the light died they saw Fergus Trayle crouched in a huddled, smoking heap at the cabinet's foot. His eyes were transfixed in a glassy stare and his body had been burned as though a bolt of lightning had indeed struck him.

At the same instant Kane ran towards the fire and snatched up the shotgun. He turned it on Cosmo.

"One move and you'll be as dead as he is," he said grimly.

Father John Dyball strode past them to where the Laird still knelt over Donald's body. The Laird turned a ravaged face towards him.

"We were too late . . ." he muttered brokenly. "After all you did . . . we were still too late."

John Dyball dropped to his knees beside the still form. He tore open the blood-stained cassock and placed his hand inside. Then he leaned down and put his ear close to Donald's mouth.

When he looked up there was a great light in his eyes.

"God heard my first prayer, as he heard my second," he said. "The knife has pierced his chest, but not vitally . . ."

"You mean . . . he will live?" The Laird's face was transfigured.

"He will live," said Father John Dyball and his hand on the Laird's shoulder was as deeply reassuring as his voice.

Menaced by the shotgun in Kane's unrelaxing grip, Cosmo Trayle led the way back to Pritchard's house. In spite of his professed powers, he obviously did not want to challenge such a formidable weapon at close quarters.

Many of the coven had escaped, running frantically back through the darkness to where they had left their cars and roaring off through the night. But Kane was not unduly concerned. He had no doubt that whatever information he—and the police —wanted would be extracted without much difficulty from the cowering, completely demoralized Rodney Pritchard.

The unconscious bodies of Fiona and Donald had

been lifted tenderly into the Land Rover and conveyed to the house. Telephone calls had already summoned an ambulance and the police.

The Laird, looking ten years younger than when he had left the Castle, sat by his son's side, looking down into the white face into which a little color had already begun to creep. Father Dyball had rendered fist aid the moment they reached Pritchard's house and although the wound Fiona had given him was deep, it was not dangerous. Within a fortnight, Dyball averred, he would be on his feet again.

"And Fiona?" asked the Laird. "Will she be all right? I mean . . ." He could not say what was in his mind, but Father Dyball knew what he was thinking.

"You mean mentally?" he said. "I agree that the terrifying experiences she has undergone could quite understandably have turned her mind—but she is a strong, healthy girl. It's more than likely that when she recovers consciousness she will remember nothing very clearly—it will all seem like a bad dream."

"And the Trayles—they can never harm us again?" asked Sir Alastair.

"Never. Fergus is dead, and Cosmo will spend quite a long time in prison. In any case, his powers were useless without Fergus."

The Laird shivered suddenly. "It was you who saved Donald," he said. "That moment in the woods . . . you knew then that he was in the greatest danger. How did you know?"

Father Dyball smiled his warm, self-effacing smile. " 'The powers that be are ordained of God,' " he said softly.

"I think I can add something else—" It was Anne

Ashby who spoke. She had just come into the room and now she stood looking from the Laird to Father Dyball.

She said, very quietly: " 'There was a man sent from God, whose name was John.' "

"Amen to that," said Sir Alastair fervently.